THE FINAL AUDIT
and Other Stories

THE FINAL AUDIT
and Other Stories

Ronald Alexander

Hollyridge Press
Venice, California

Hollyridge Press
P.O. Box 2872
Venice, California 90294

Photos by Albert Chacon
Design by Rick Lange, Hollywood Title, Burbank, California

Manufactured in the United States of America by Lightning Print

The following stories have been published previously, all copyrights
in the name of the author: "The Final Audit" originally appeared in
New Mexico Humanities Review; "Beautiful Carpets" appeared in *The
James White Review*; "The Earl" appeared in *Confrontation*.

Publisher's Cataloging-in-Publication
(Provided by Quality Books, Inc.)

Alexander, Ronald Dennis.
    The final audit and other stories / Ronald
Alexander. -- 1st American pbk. ed.
    p. cm.
    LCCN: 99-91653
    ISBN: 0-9676003-1-6

    I. Title.

PS3551.L546F56 1999   813.54
                    QBI99-500584

First American Paperback Edition

09 08 07 06 05 04 03 02 01 00   10 9 8 7 6 5 4 3 2 1

In memory of Albert Chacon.

How dare you smile like that! No one is allowed to smile like that!

—Thomas Mann, *Death in Venice*

Contents

With thanks to my family for their love and to Chris Harvey for his support.

Thanks also to Reginald Gibbons, whose encouragement and suggestions helped to turn a group of disparate stories into a collection.

The Final Audit

In six weeks Dexter Giles would be finished with the Philippines, finished with the audit, finished with Imperial Petroleum, and finished with Norbert Steinhoff.

Perspiration trickled down his spine. His shirt clung to his skin, and wet circles appeared at the armpits of his blue, pinstriped suit of worsted wool, but he didn't remove his jacket. He did remove his wire-rimmed glasses, to mop his cheeks and brow, because the salt in his perspiration burned his eyes. It seemed ironic to him—the perfect finish to a disappointing career—that he should have to come to such an impoverished, inaccessible region on his last audit before retirement. Including the layover in Tokyo, the flight from Chicago to Manila had taken twenty-three hours. He had hoped for a final assignment in northern Italy or the North Sea—where the food and customs were less exotic and the political environment was more stable.

He stood, exhausted, next to the exit in the faint breeze, away from the herd of people positioning themselves for their luggage. Airports were worse than bus stations these days: the crowds were larger.

A stabbing sensation at the top of his calf suddenly buckled his left knee.

"Sorry, Mister." The small woman in the soiled blouse peered at him as if she expected to be struck. She had bumped him with her suitcase—a flimsy cardboard affair held together loosely with rope that allowed pieces of washed-out material to stick through the seams. With a flick of his wrist Dexter waved her past, and after she had shuffled away he shook his head wondering where such a ragged creature had procured the funds for air travel.

Outside, jeepney drivers solicited passengers for the ride into the city, and he stepped through the door to get a closer look. It had been over forty years since the American military abandoned these jeeps at the end of the war, nearly half a century since the natives appropriated them for public transportation, but most of them were still in service. Dexter couldn't imagine where they got replacement parts for these contraptions, then grunted, thinking about the sad state of the American automobile industry.

"Hey, you need a fast ride into the city?" The man smiled, exposing an upper row of gold teeth. With a sweeping gesture, he pointed to a garish station wagon— orange and green with silver trim. Yellow lights adorned the flat surfaces, there were hand-painted designs and slogans on the side panels, and a smooth spare tire without the memory of a tread rested on the running board. Dexter counted nine people already inside. Despite a preponderant sun, rain began to fall in heavy, swollen drops from patchy, black clouds, as the driver stepped toward him. Other drivers, mistakenly assuming that a contract was about to be made, also moved forward, prompting Dexter to hurry back into the airport.

Being a full head above the plain of brown faces facilitated his search for Steinhoff, who had insisted on meeting him. In fact, when Dexter made the transoceanic call, to discuss the details of his impending arrival in the Philippines, he had been so surprised by Steinhoff's cordiality that he had failed to say anything for several seconds. In his thirty-three years as an auditor for Imperial, this was his first trip to the Orient, but not his first experience with Norbert Steinhoff.

"Christ, Giles, what the hell you doing in a damn suit? I'll bet you dress for dinner too."

Dexter turned, certain that Steinhoff had come from behind to confuse him. "It was chilly when I left Chicago."

"We'll have to fix you up with some barongs," said Steinhoff. He clenched his cigar between his teeth, stretched his arms, and turned, displaying his pastel blue shirt with short sleeves: a garment embellished with embroidered patterns that fit tightly around his obese stomach. It looked to Dexter like a pharmacist's coat.

"Do you like slant-eyed pussy, Giles?"

"Excuse me."

"Do you like Oriental women? This is the real Disneyland. Filipino girls love American men."

"I think I see my luggage," Dexter said.

***

Inside his eighth floor room in the Hotel Intercontinental, there was little to remind Dexter that he was 8,159 statute miles from home, on the other side of the world. The bed, king-sized, had a slightly soiled beige spread on it, the television included cable and American movies, the desk drawer was loaded with stationery, and the bathroom included the standard basket of toiletries: several bars of soap, hand and body lotion, shampoo, conditioner, a shoe cleaning cloth, and an undersized plastic shower cap trimmed with inferior quality elastic.

His inventory also revealed that he had only one hand towel and no wash cloths, so he penciled a note for housekeeping. Other than that, things in the room were as they should be. As long as he stayed in a newer hotel, he could usually sleep as well as he might in Houston, Texas or Cheyenne, Wyoming—or in his one-bedroom apartment that overlooked Lincoln Park back in Chicago. It took a few nights to adjust to the particular noises and specific characteristics of a room. In Salt Lake City, the air was so dry he had to throw ice buckets of water on the carpeting to prevent the violent static shocks he received when he touched metal; in Cairo, the air conditioning vents rattled until he stuffed strips of newspaper between the metal slats; in Glasgow, he had to purchase a portable electric heater to remove the chill from the room. Generally, it took a night or two to identify the problem, and a night or two to fix it. The number of time zones he crossed determined how long it took to adjust to the jet lag, so Manila might be a problem. It was still Saturday night in Chicago, but here, it was Sunday afternoon.

Broad, palm-lined avenues crisscrossed the area below: Makati. This affluent district of office towers, condominiums, and hotels had temporarily been seized by rebel army forces less than a year ago, but things appeared normal now; he could hear the noise of traffic through the glass. Beyond Makati were narrower streets and modest buildings of one and two stories. Beyond that, barely visible, were the tin-roofed shanties they had driven past on their way in from the airport.

Here in the Philippines, Norbert Steinhoff occupied the top position: Director of Exploration and Production. Twenty years ago, when they first met, he'd been in charge of Materials Procurement at the Company's Houston refinery, and if it hadn't been for that one invoice, Dexter might never have caught on to him. The very next day, after he'd called the supplier with his questions, Steinhoff invited him home for dinner. That's when Dexter asked Mrs. Steinhoff about the fresh wallpaper in the den.

"Thank you. Yes, I just had it done. Call me Shirley. Would you care for a salty dog? It's vodka and grapefruit juice." She licked her upper lip and winked. "They're scrumptious."

Dexter studied Mrs. Steinhoff's teased coiffure, black as shoe polish. He couldn't recall having ever seen a middle-aged woman with so much hair, and her earrings were so large they brushed against the shoulders of her dress when she laughed.

None of the refinery offices were papered, and he had covered the conflict of interest in his audit report to management who, after careful consideration, reprimanded Steinhoff and promoted him to Trinidad where he lived better than the British had in India.

Dexter returned to the bed and began to unpack. Since six weeks had been allocated for the audit of accounts payable documents and drilling progress reports, he had packed exactly forty-two pairs of boxer shorts and undershirts. Hotel laundries in foreign countries were notorious for their failure to use fabric softener, and with his propensity for rashes he couldn't take a chance on the services in a place like this. He arranged the underwear neatly in the bureau drawer, then took the silver-framed picture of his two Abyssinians from his suitcase and placed it on the desk in front of the mirror.

***

A thin, crisply-dressed woman with a broad, flat nose came into the lobby and extended her hand. "Mr. Steinhoff is on the telephone to Chicago at the moment. I'm his secretary. Rose Santana. Would you like a cup of coffee while you wait?"

"No thank you. If you could show me the office I'll be using."

"Mr. Steinhoff wants to show you around. Are you sure? We have decaffeinated."

Dexter watched her disappear through the doors, then stooped to check the contents of his audit bag. Number two lead pencils, thirteen-column spread sheets, erasers, paper clips, a stapler, the corporate audit manual, a comb, a lint brush—and the magazine. The boy's face leered up at him. Dexter had forgotten to leave the magazine at the hotel. He withdrew the key from his vest pocket, locked the bag, and straightened. Buttoning his suit coat, he glanced at the receptionist, and was relieved to see her occupied with a telephone call. He went to the louvered window that overlooked Quezon Street, moved his neck from side to side and forward to relieve the stiffness. The company doctor had prescribed Naprocyn, but after the long plane ride and a sleepless night, the 375 milligram tablets were not lessening the soreness.

There was a Honda dealership across the street and next to it a Suzuki service center. Japanese automobiles were everywhere: in the show rooms, in traffic, parked. The only exceptions were the loaded jeepneys which clattered past. A skinny yellow dog, its tail curved backwards in a circle, dodged one such vehicle to cross the street. The dog glanced up at him, lifted its leg, and peed on the curb before continuing his journey. It baffled Dexter that stray dogs always seemed so sure of where they were going.

"Mr. Stein-hoff will see you now," the receptionist called. She pronounced the two syllables distinctly, as if they were separate names and somehow incongruous. "Through these doors, and to your right."

The tension on the metal-framed glass door was adjusted too tightly, and the door slammed shut on the heavy audit bag before Dexter could pull it through. The motion stretched his neck painfully, and he yelled: "Damn! Who's the monkey in charge of maintenance?"

"Having a little trouble this morning?" Dexter looked around to see Steinhoff's stomach encased in a lemon-yellow barong. He had come from his office to greet Dexter and stood silently while he struggled to free the audit bag. "I expected you an hour ago." Steinhoff smiled. "We start work at eight o'clock." Dexter brushed past Steinhoff and around the partition that shielded the work area from reception. The room, large and open, was arranged in rows of desks occupied by Filipinos. The noise of their calculators ceased when Dexter burst into the room, and the workers looked up. "This is our accounting department," Steinhoff said. He raised his voice. "Everyone, if I could have your attention for a moment. This is the auditor from Chicago. He'll be checking to make sure y'all are doing a good job."

Dexter felt the beginning of a sinus headache. The windows on the street side of the office were open, and the air was heavy with mold. Ceiling fans seemed barely to turn. Dexter cleared his throat. "As President Harry Truman once said, the buck stops at the top." A young man at the first desk smiled, and Dexter nodded an acknowledgment. Addressing Steinhoff, he said: "Perhaps you could show me where I'll be stationed."

Steinhoff's expression hardened. "We're a little short of space, you'll have to work at a table in the employee lunch room. Manny, show him where it is." The boy who had smiled jumped to his feet.

***

The lobby of the Intercontinental was a cavernous, two story affair, filled with lounge furniture and tropical plants. Except for a few businessmen though, and a bored-looking pianist playing "Raindrops" on a baby grand in one corner, the space was deserted. One man, a Westerner, sat isolated on a sofa reading a book, and a group of four Japanese men sat together around a coffee table loaded with cocktails and filled ashtrays. They laughed and talked among themselves until a fifth man approached, at which point they rose and began to bow energetically. They paid no attention as Dexter passed.

He wasn't sure how far away from the hotel he should venture—Steinhoff had warned that army rebels, communists, and Muslims were only a few of the dangers, and that anti-American sentiments were on the rise—but he thought a walk might relax his stomach. The meat in the hotel dining room tasted gamy and all he could think about were the strange smells in the hot lunch room where he had worked all day. People had offered him food throughout the day, but Steinhoff also told him Filipinos ate dog meat, joking that they ate a delicacy named *Queenie Almondine*. He didn't believe they would serve dog at an Intercontinental, but after one bite all he felt he could keep down was something the waitress called *pan de sal*.

The street in front of the hotel was lined with idle taxis, and the drivers parked closest to the entrance began immediately to seek his business. Dexter kept repeating: "No. No. No." To the left, he saw a building with an enormous NCR sign on the roof, and to the right, one that said Toyota. The immediate area appeared safe, so he decided to go toward the NCR building, since it was an

American company. He saw some flowering shrubs with pink blooms that he was curious about as well.

As he approached the shrubs, a boy came out from among some trees on the opposite side of the street and walked towards him. Dexter didn't stop to examine the pink buds, but increased his pace.

"You are looking for someone, Mister."

"No."

"You are looking for a woman perhaps."

"No." The sidewalk sloped uphill, and Dexter began to perspire.

"Where are you from, Mister?"

"The U.S."

"I have cousins in Los Angeles, Mister. Where do you come from in the United States?" the boy said.

Dexter slowed a bit and glanced at the boy. He looked about fifteen. He had clean, healthy looking black hair; Dexter imagined his skin was quite soft. "Chicago. I live in Chicago," he said.

"Rattatatatat." The boy laughed and held his hands as if they cradled a machine gun.

"Yes, I know." Dexter smiled at the boy. He could be from Costa Rica were it not for his almond-shaped Oriental eyes.

"You are looking for a boy, Mister? Do you like me, Mister?"

***

All week Dexter had difficulty sitting up straight in the plastic chair with the metal legs; it was shaped like a soup ladle and he kept sliding to the middle. The heat from the vending machines and his backache made it especially difficult to concentrate on this particular morning, as he bent over his green-lined work sheet. He had chosen a large sample of invoices to review—more than a hundred and fifty. Normally, the tedious itemization of specifics was a favorite task. He enjoyed seeing patterns emerge: how long on average it took to pay a bill, who the big vendors were, whether or not the expenditure seemed reasonable.

At the opposite end of the lunch room three girls from the accounting department were having their morning coffee break, speaking Tagalog, an odd and distracting dialect, the sounds emanating from the head and nose rather than the chest. The women alternately chattered and whispered, and, occasionally, giggled. Dexter scowled at them.

He took the pocket calendar from his jacket and crossed off the first week, one day at a time, using a red felt marking pen. "It's a little early to be counting the days, isn't it?" Steinhoff slapped Dexter on the back.

Dexter threw the marking pen into the air. "Don't you ever knock?" He twisted his head until his neck cracked, and tightened his tie.

"Didn't mean to scare you. Let's get together at five-thirty so you can bring me up to date on the audit." He made as if to leave, then hesitated. "How are the accommodations working out?"

"Fine," Dexter lied. He removed his glasses, fogged them with his breath, and polished them with his handkerchief.

"Listen," said Steinhoff. "Manny's going to Baguio on vacation next week. I'm sure he wouldn't mind if you used his desk while he's gone." Again he started to leave, then added: "You should get a driver and go up there some weekend. To Baguio, I mean. It's beautiful. Or better yet, go up to Banaue and see the rice terraces. There's not a spot on earth more beautiful."

***

Norbert Steinhoff's office was air-conditioned. The window behind him held a large, powerful casement model that kept the room chilly. The space itself, though, was much too small to accommodate the credenza and the giant walnut desk and the high-backed leather chair. Steinhoff had photographs of his daughters next to a vase of stale flowers; the girls had narrow, acned faces and chemically-damaged hair parted in the middle, which in Dexter's opinion, caused them to resemble Afghan hounds. Next to them was a picture of the girl's mother standing on the veranda of the house in Trinidad.

Steinhoff had managed oil production activities on the island, and Dexter recalled how the man had thrived there as an expatriate, in spite of the languid humidity. The house had perched on a mountaintop, overlooking the sea: a mansion Steinhoff called "Tara of the Caribbean," staffed with plenty of servants.

"We have a full-time cook, two housekeepers, and a gardener all for less money than we shelled out for a once-a-week cleaning woman in Houston." Steinhoff had itemized them on his fingers, using exaggerated gestures, the smoke from his cigar encircling their heads.

"That must be quite helpful to you, Mrs. Steinhoff," Dexter said taking a step backward.

"Honey, please call me Shirley. Cocktail before dinner? I'm having a rum and Coke." She looked at the shiny black girl and added: "Lots of ice, right?" The girl nodded, handed her the tall glass, and disappeared into the kitchen.

Later in the evening, after dinner and several more cocktails, which became progressively paler, Shirley Steinhoff had confided with fermented tears: "There's nothing for me to do, but eat and gain weight. The girls are in school in the States, and I hate golf. Norbert has his job, but I don't have any friends here. There's no place to shop, there are no good movies, and one darned television station. My God, I've read *Madame Bovary* three times." Then Steinhoff came back into the room, and she was silent.

Back at the office in Port-of-Spain, Dexter found all of the household employees on the Company payroll. He disclosed the expenditure violations in *Exhibit I* of the audit report, Steinhoff was demoted to Cairo, and that was where, only three years ago, the unfortunate incident had taken place.

The harsh rays of the Philippine sun streamed through the window above the air conditioner. The slice of light progressed slowly until it shined directly in Dexter's eyes and backlit Norbert Steinhoff, making the features of his face indistinguishable. Steinhoff leaned back in his chair; it jammed against the credenza. For ten minutes now the man had been looking through half-spectacles at a memorandum while Dexter waited in the chair across from him.

"Perhaps you'd like me to come back next week."

"I'm sorry, Giles. It's this damn memo from the general office. They don't have any idea what it's like to do business in the Orient." He took a long cigar from a wooden humidor trimmed in brass. "Cigar?" He held one out to Dexter.

"No. Thank you."

Steinhoff lit it himself, turned and took two glasses from the credenza, and set them on his desk pad. Without a glance at Dexter, he took a bottle of Wild Turkey from a lower desk drawer and poured a shot in each glass. "To the Philippines," he said raising the glass in grandiloquent fashion. Without matching his enthusiasm, Dexter raised his glass and drank.

"This is the goddamnest place I've ever been," Norbert Steinhoff began. "If your house catches on fire, you've got to line the fireman's palms with *pesos* before he'll hook up the blasted hose. If your house is robbed, they won't fill out a report till you've made it worth their while... Do you know what I'm talking about, Giles?"

"Not exactly..."

"There are certain expenses of doing business here, certain entertainment expenses... The customs here are such that— "

"Company procedures outline with a high degree of specificity those expenses which are allowable. I'm afraid IRS regulations are also quite specific." Dexter took another swallow of whiskey.

"Naturally. But if you have any questions during your review, if anything seems unusual, I would hope you would come to me first. I'm sure there's a reason behind all our expenditures. The Filipinos work like beavers, they're damn good workers."

"Yes?"

"As you know, our drilling is done by contractors."

"What's your point?"

"I believe we can avoid the unpleasant situation that arose during the audit in Egypt."

Dexter felt a surge of blood in his temples and his ears rang as if the air pressure in the room had unexpectedly changed. "I see," he managed to respond.

"If you would only learn to work with me instead of sneaking back to Chicago with your confidential reports. We both know people make mistakes. *To err is human.*"

"I tried to discuss my findings with you."

"Let's not open old wounds. This is a new job, your last job. It would be a shame for anything to mess up your pension. Listen, why not let me take you to dinner, to celebrate your retirement."

"Actually, I—"

"I won't take no for an answer. I'll pick you up at the hotel at eight."

***

French doors lined the far wall of the room. Through the glass, Dexter saw a lush flower garden and several stone benches. Flanking the doors on the inside were enormous urns with palms that touched the ceiling. Three chandeliers lit the room with an amber warmth. White jacketed waiters stood at attention, coming to life whenever a diner beckoned. A string quartet struggled through Mozart.

"Do you like history, Giles?"

"I prefer science," he replied. Steinhoff slumped across from him in the green leather banquette. His grey eyes were bloodshot and his lids drooped. He wore a pink barong with long sleeves, this one fit him better than the ones he wore to the office. Dexter pulled the cuffs of his white shirt over his wrists, smoothed his silk paisley tie, and unbuttoned his coat.

"Mac had his headquarters right here in the Hotel Manila. Top floor. He lived like a goddamn potentate. How things change." He laughed to emphasize his remark. "You know, you could go to Corregidor while you're here. Course the Japs swarm over the place like locusts."

I'm afraid I only have enough time allocated for the audit review."

"What about the weekend. What do you do on weekends?" The waiter refilled Dexter's wine glass, then Steinhoff's.

"I read."

"We're ready to order now. What's that, Giles?"

"Books," Dexter replied. "I read books."

"Hey, me too. I like that King fella." Steinhoff lit a cigar. "Read one about this car that was haunted. I think I used to own that car. A LeBaron... with crushed velvet upholstery. Fancier than the inside of a damn coffin." He laughed louder and his cigar smoke hung over the table, motionless.

"Are those things like the Filipinos' answer to the leisure suit?"

"Huh?"

"Your barong." Dexter emphasized the *gee*.

"Now that you mention it, kind of like that. Shirley bought me this one." He finished his wine. "She thought the pink was dressy."

An image of Shirley Steinhoff came to Dexter's mind. At the dinner in Houston, she had worn a muumuu. "Where is Mrs. Steinhoff?"

"Back in Texas with her mom. I'm afraid all is not well on the home front. I'll tell you about it when we go out for a nightcap."

"Oh no. I've got to get back after dinner." He looked at his watch. "It's already ten-thirty."

"Dexter, drink up and shut up." He raised his glass and removed his cigar. "To Pilipino poontang," he toasted.

***

Rain had turned the unpaved shoulder of the road to mud. The front wheel of the Mercedes sedan slipped into a hole, sending a spray of dirty water past Dexter's open window, and twice Steinhoff went off the road, only managing to get the car back on course with several violent turns of the steering wheel, as the lip between the road and the apron was quite high. There were no street lights in this section of the city. A full moon illuminated the surroundings—when it wasn't hidden behind one of the dense rain clouds scattered across the sky.

On Dexter's right a barangay of shabby housing sat protected and isolated by industrial fencing—ten feet high and anchored in concrete. Immediately behind the fence was a paved recreation area with a net-less basketball hoop and beyond this lay hundreds of houses wedged improbably together. There was no consistency of color or materials in the design of these structures to tell where one house left off and another began. Only occasionally did he see a patch of color, a weak yellow, a bleached blue. Sheets of rusted, corrugated tin covered scraps of weathered lumber; tattered clothing hung on makeshift clotheslines; primitive, uncomplicated television antennae sprouted from the roofs like weeds. During the past week, Dexter had been surprised at the suddenness of the heavy winds and rain that had come frequently without warning. Meager housing like this would be flattened during the monsoon.

Steinhoff broke the silence. "Shit, this is plush. They got people living in the garbage down by the bay. They call it Smoky Mountain. It breaks your heart."

"I insist you take me back to my hotel," Dexter said. The air held so much moisture; it seemed to him that it would begin to rain at any moment.

"Enjoy yourself for once." Steinhoff burped.

They entered an area with intermittent street lights, and traffic signals which were suspended over the intersections. When one such signal abruptly changed from green to red—there was no yellow stage in between for caution—Steinhoff skidded to a halt, and the car slid sideways on the gravel-covered concrete. For an instant Dexter had feared he would not bother to stop at all in his drunken state. As they waited for the green, children and adults swarmed upon the car like insects to beg for pesos, and a dirty arm, covered in bursting sores, snaked in through Dexter's window, the hand undulating in his face. The beggar's splayed fingers expanded and contracted like the legs of a dying beetle. Dexter put his window up.

"Where is this place?" he asked.

"Not far." Steinhoff had developed hiccups and his body convulsed with turbulence as he gripped the steering wheel with one hand and an unlit cigar with the other. "Relax," he said, "the neighborhood gets a little better."

Shortly thereafter, Steinhoff pulled into a muddy lot next to a long, wooden, two-story building. Five teenaged boys descended on the car, but he waved them away. "We know where to go, boys. Let us through."

Dexter stepped around the puddles and trailed Steinhoff up rickety stairs on the outside of the building and into a darkened barroom. The space was practically devoid of decor; the unpainted wood walls soaked up most of the sickly light radiating from the single bulb that dangled from the ceiling. There were two rusted metal tables with chairs, but the focal point of the room was a bar and three stools against the far wall where three unescorted women sat together drinking beer from bottles and smoking. A display of liquors graced the wall behind the bar. One of the women, a squat, primitive creature in pink lipstick, smiled at Dexter. He moved his shoulders rapidly in a circular shrugging motion to relieve the itching under his arms, and checked his coat pocket to make sure he still had his medicine.

"*Buenas noches, Señor Steinhoff.*" The proprietor, an older Filipino man, dressed in a white one-piece suit, entered. "Everything is prepared." He led them down a darkened corridor, past several doors, and into a narrow room, which unlike the barroom and the hallway, was bright, fluorescent white, its walls draped in faded, red fabric. A bench the length of the room was fastened against the far wall, and a few feet from the bench anchored against the opposing wall was a bed-sized platform upholstered in red vinyl.

Steinhoff grinned. "Iced tea." He clapped his hands and stumbled off-balance, still wrestling with his hiccups.

The Filipino smiled, put his hand on Steinhoff's shoulder, and replied: "Already ordered. *Por favor, sientese.* Make yourself comfortable."

"I taught them how to make Long Island iced tea," Steinhoff said to Dexter, when the girl, balancing two drinks on a plastic tray, appeared. She was followed by a younger girl, about fifteen, and an older woman of indeterminable age, both of whom wore satin weave robes. Once the drinks were distributed, the barmaid left, closing the door behind her. Dexter took great gulps to empty his glass, in the hope that he could adjust to the mingled odors of sour alcohol and perspiration permeating the room.

"Let the show begin," Steinhoff called, waving his arms. The bench sagged under his weight with a splintering sound. The girl and woman dropped their robes and, now naked, approached him. The older woman, heavier about the arms and shoulders and with short cropped hair, turned the young girl around and directed her to sit between Steinhoff's legs so that her back rested against his chest and stomach. Straddling her like that, and with a face more flushed than usual, he began to pinch her nipples between his thumbs and forefingers. The child sat impassively until the woman dropped to her knees and began licking the girl's navel, slowly following the trail of light hair to her vagina. As she probed her with her tongue, Steinhoff sipped his drink. The room became a vacuum, swallowing sound.

Without taking his eyes off the three, Dexter inched backwards until he was trapped in a far corner. The dinner and wine seethed in his stomach, and he feared that if he didn't relax he might have to make a dash for the toilet, an undesirable prospect in such surroundings. When he sat down, the woman got to her feet and led the girl by the arm to him.

"Oh no," Dexter shouted. Jumping up, he kicked a beer bottle across the sticky linoleum floor. A cockroach flew off and disappeared into a crack at the base of the wall.

"Christ, Giles," Steinhoff grumbled. "Don't be such a pussy." He clapped his hands. "More action."

The man in white waved the older woman to the door and stood in the opening frantically motioning until a lean, glabrous boy, clad only in a towel, entered. The adolescent dropped the towel and approached the girl, who seemed more enthusiastic with this pairing, lying at once on her back in the middle of the platform. As the youth mounted her, Steinhoff moved up close, arms akimbo, mumbled something about the boy being hard, and grinned. From his spot on the bench, Dexter watched the muscles in the boy's hips and buttocks contracting and flexing as he made immediate love to the girl; his cheeks were smooth and brown like the rest of his body. When Dexter shifted his eyes to Steinhoff, he confirmed a suspicion that instead of observing the two lovers, the man was regarding him; his unsavory smile glaring in the harsh light of the airless room. Dexter dropped his eyes to the floor, and was perturbed to discover his best shoes caked in mud.

"*Gago! Pinapaalis mo ang magaling* customer," the man in white yelled. The boy got up from the platform; judging from the look of embarrassment on his face, Dexter gathered that he had been unable to delay his orgasm. The boy held his hands in front of his genitals, as if he had only that moment discovered his nudity, when the enraged man shoved him from the room. Dexter glowered at the proprietor stationed once more at the door, shouting yet again his instructions down the hall. He imagined himself jumping at the man, tearing the styleless, white suit from his wrinkled, sagging body and forcing him at knife point to dance a gross and humiliating dance up on the platform. He would push his sickening face in the crotch of the first woman and make him perform like a trained dog.

The barmaid placed two drinks on the bench, and pulled on Dexter's sleeve. With concerned eyes, she said: "I am very sorry. He is a young toro. He does not put on a good show. This man is a good toro. He is our best toro." A short, thickly-built man had entered the room.

Dexter pulled free from her grasp and sat down. He gazed at the man's back and arms—thinking that it must have taken a long time to get so many tattoos, and wondering if the young boy would end up like this: vile and mutilated.

"These guys get a tattoo every time they're in prison," Steinhoff slurred.

The toro wasted no time. Like a mongrel, he dominated the girl, relentlessly pounding her. Steinhoff watched with apparent delight. As her young body slapped against the platform, Dexter studied the dirty soles of the man's feet, the placement of his tattoos, and the lack of expression on the girl's face as her head jutted rhythmically against the wall.

"Do you like the show?" The barmaid suddenly grabbed Dexter's crotch, and angrily he pushed her away. The slapping, grunting, groaning got faster, louder, more intense. And monotonous. This man was having as much difficulty achieving an orgasm as the young man had had postponing his. At last, he climaxed and pulled out, whereupon he strutted across the room, tore a piece of fabric off the wall, and wiped his penis. When he was finished, he dropped the material to the floor, and started toward Dexter. Dexter immediately sat forward from the wall and arose.

The barmaid grasped Dexter's trouser pockets. "You have pesos for me? You liked the show?"

Dexter struggled past her and the man to the door, where Steinhoff was attempting conversation with the man in white, who in turn pointed at the young girl. "May we go now?" Dexter interrupted.

Steinhoff turned to him. He wore an expression Dexter did not recognize. When he opened his mouth to speak, his jaw moved sideways, not up and down. He gestured over his shoulder and managed a smile, but remained silent.

"Yes, have your fun," Dexter said. "She's much prettier than your daughters... and she probably smells better."

***

The rain fell with increasing intensity, but Dexter couldn't run any further. He had twisted his ankle when he fell into the ditch. An insane picture of that time at the Marriott in Cairo kept recurring in his mind when he landed face down in the water. The fear that there were probably snakes in the tall grass and water left him no choice but to walk up on the road. He had to risk being seen. Besides, at this point nothing looked familiar. He had retraced the route as far as he could remember. Nothing was familiar. His suit was ruined. Even his body seemed not his own.

It had happened so fast. It was difficult to recall the exact sequence of events. Despite his effort to back out of the way, Steinhoff had caught him by the lapel. So fast. The ripping sound of his favorite suit, the wrenching pain in his back when the weight of Steinhoff's body slammed him against the wall, the guttural sounds Steinhoff finally made, as he stared hatefully into Dexter's eyes, the young girl's screams, the macabre dance the two men did as Dexter tried to loosen his attacker's fleshy hands from his coat. Then he covered his eyes, tried to protect his glasses, was aware of people rushing into the room, but the blows he expected never came. Other people came, the girl's screams were combined with deeper voices, other men, other females. Scuffling sounds in the hall, doors slamming, running, the pain in Dexter's temples, then the fingers letting go. The weight was gone. Then silence, mumbling, confused conversation, until it built again, higher and higher. Then the screams again. Dexter opened his eyes. Steinhoff looked at him from the floor. Eyes open but unfocused.

The headlights from the rear grew brighter. Ahead, Dexter saw streetlights and an area more heavily inhabited. He couldn't run. He turned toward the approaching vehicle. The rain washed over his face. The car pulled alongside and slowed.

He had never seen a dead man before. He'd seen dead people in coffins, but he'd never seen anyone freshly dead. And Steinhoff was dead. Unexperienced as he was, Dexter knew dead when he saw it. Steinhoff was dead. He knew when he first saw him there on the floor, ash gray and rigid. And he knew it when he stepped away from the wall and over the body and into the hall. He knew it when he ran from the bar, down the steps and across the parking lot and into the driving rain and gusting wind.

"*Luko-loco ka ba? Anong ginagawa mo sa bagyo?*" the driver of the jeepney yelled.

"Take me to the Intercontinental?" Dexter yelled back over the noise of the storm.

"*Sí, sí, Señor. Delawang pesos.*" He pointed to the back.

Soaked, Dexter limped to the rear of the jeepney and struggled inside. A bolt of lightning lit the sky. A scrofulous woman and four small children huddled together like mice, close to the front, away from the rain.

***

Sprawled on the bathroom floor next to the toilet, Dexter tried to tell himself it was the shrimp he'd had for dinner. But the shrimp had come up right after the Long Island iced teas and he still didn't feel any better. It was as if his abdomen was stretched tightly over a sack of gravel. He struggled to his feet, flushed the toilet again and turned on the cold water at the sink. His skin felt sore to the touch and he was sweating harder now. He held the cool wash cloth against his eyes and forehead for a minute and decided to try again to rest in bed. He took the chocolate from the pillow, tossed it in the wastebasket, and pulled the blanket back.

He wondered how much money was involved here. The payments he had uncovered in Egypt revealed how well Steinhoff had been compensated for his influence in the Middle East—the bank in Cairo had showed its appreciation for the Imperial account by making consulting fee payments in excess of $100,000. And Dexter had had no choice but to let him get away with it. There was no telling how much Steinhoff had received here in the Philippines for seeing that invoices from the drilling contractors were approved without question.

Suddenly chilled, he pulled the blanket up to his chin. If he had only double-locked the door at the Marriott, Steinhoff would not have been able to gain entry with the pass key he'd bribed the desk clerk for. He began to shiver under the blanket and covered his head now as well. There hadn't been any time he'd been so completely taken by surprise. He hadn't even heard the door open. Then the room was flooded in light and there he was not ten feet from the bed. He must have been a ludicrous sight on his hands and knees like that.

"This is my room," Dexter had screamed. "Get out!" He tried to hide himself with the sheet and reached for the robe he had discarded on the chair next to the bed.

Steinhoff leered like a duelist who had just knocked the sword from his opponent's hand. "You must like that little Arab boy, Giles," he yelled. "You're stiff as a board."

***

Shirley Steinhoff had aged. Chemically coloring her hair, black as ever, accentuated the heavy lines in her face; applying eye shadow and mascara highlighted the dark swelling around her eyes; smearing lipstick beyond the lip lines emphasized their thinness.

"Honey, he was very unhappy at first," she said. She leaned back on the sectional sofa clutching her glass of Southern Comfort. "We found this apartment right after Norbert was transferred to Manila. I'd never lived in a high rise before." She looked around the living room, nostalgically, it seemed to Dexter.

"It's kind of like an ant farm," Dexter said.

Shirley Steinhoff looked confused. "Beg your pardon?" she said.

"Living in a tall building. It's like living in an ant farm."

She frowned, paused, then continued. "Poor Norbert didn't want to look around; he took the first thing the agent showed us. He thought he should have had a staff position in Chicago, you know. Course he never complained... He told everyone the Cubs were going to move with him to the Philippines and they were going to rename them the Manila Folders." She laughed lightly, then began to dab at the corners of her eyes with a cocktail napkin. "But he really started liking this place. He really liked the people. He said they'd been through so much—"

"How long will you be staying in Manila?" Dexter inquired.

"Well, I must arrange to have Norbert's body shipped home, I have to close up the apartment; fortunately, I had most of our things sent back when I left him... Did Norbert tell you I left him?"

"He said something to that effect."

"Did he tell you why?"

"No, I'm afraid not. I should be getting back to the office. I still have to finish the audit and issue—"

"I caught him, right here in our house, with the housekeeper. She was just a girl. Boy, did I get that little bitch's ass out of here fast." Shirley Steinhoff looked angry. "I should have suspected something when he got those French uniforms for her. He never took any interest in the servants before." Her expression softened. "I understand you had dinner with him that evening."

Dexter sipped his wine. "Yes. He wanted to take me out to celebrate my retirement. We went to the Manila Hotel."

"Oh, Norbert's favorite. So elegant. Isn't it beautiful?"

"Yes. Lovely. Then he drove me back to my hotel."

"And that's the last you saw of him?"

"Yes, till, they called the office... for an identification. He hadn't been to work for several days. Rose said he'd gone to Palawan, but when he didn't return -"

"And they were certain it was a heart attack? Norbert was a little overweight, and he did smoke those cigars... But what was he doing driving down by the bay?"

"He'd been drinking and was lost, apparently. They found him slumped over the wheel on Smoky Mountain—"

"The dump?"

"He'd been stripped of all his valuables. They stripped the car too, but left the registration. No one reported it for a week. The body had already started decomposing by the time someone notified the authorities, and it goes without saying the place is infested with rats."

Shirley Steinhoff paled and covered her mouth.

"The registration showed the car belonged to Imperial," Dexter continued. "That's what prompted the authorities to call the office. He was practically naked, and covered with flies. A person has to pull the flies off his face when he walks the streets, so you can imagine what it was like at Smoky Mountain."

"Oh Jesus, Mary and Joseph," Shirley Steinhoff wailed.

"I was able to identify him from his barong. For some reason no one had taken it off him. It was pink. He had worn it to dinner that evening—"

"He was wearing the barong I gave him. The barong I gave him." She began to sob convulsively. "His beautiful barong. His beautiful barong," she keened.

Dexter glanced around the apartment. A floor to ceiling stack of open shelving served as a room divider separating the living and dining areas. The shelves contained very few books. There were photos of the Steinhoff family; the daughters had been captured at various stages of their development; there were curios and mementos of Norbert Steinhoff's career; there were vases of artificial flowers; there were stacks of records; lots of video tapes; and a collection of miniature ceramic chickens. A large, beige recliner sat next to the divider; it was placed directly in front of the television and video recorder. The room was covered with olive-green shag carpeting, and the furniture was cheap and tasteless as well. The sofa shook under the weight of Shirley Steinhoff's lowing. Dexter crossed his legs and contemplated her ensemble. She wore a white tent-like dress with large black spots. She was dressed like a Holstein. Behind her, the sliding glass doors to the balcony were opened, allowing the noise of Makati rush hour traffic to drift up into the room.

The stiffness in Dexter's neck had abated. Even his sinuses felt pretty good. He missed his babies though. They were highly intelligent cats. They sulked when he was gone, punished him for awhile after he returned. He hoped the boarders were taking proper care of them. After this audit, he wouldn't have to leave them again. He should be back at the office, working. Once he finished his analysis, he could begin the draft of the final report. The report would be easier this time. There would be no excuses, no apologies. Nothing to stop him from disclosing the payments, the waste, the greed, the lack of principles. Nothing to stop him from expressing his opinion that Steinhoff had been ethically and morally unsuited for any executive position.

Shirley Steinhoff had quieted somewhat. She took a big swallow of her drink and snuffed her nose. Dexter looked out onto the balcony behind her. A light breeze whistled through the fronds of a large, potted palm, and the sun, now golden, neared the horizon. It promised to be a perfect evening for a walk.

Beautiful Carpets

Not until he was on the boat, making the crossing from Algeciras to Tangier, did Dexter Giles have second thoughts about Morocco. He had arisen early, in time to make the morning hovercraft, and the air was still cool; the sun was only now rising behind Gibraltar. He sniffed aloud. The rock had all the charm of a strip mall. Without the monkeys the place would be totally lacking in appeal. And the food. One would think living so close to Portugal and Morocco that the English might have learned something about spices, but the food was as dreadful as in Leeds or Manchester.

Jean Paul had invited him, writing about the bargains to be found in Tangier and it was purely coincidence that Dexter needed a carpet, a runner for his hallway. Of course Jean Paul had written about the Moroccan boys too, not bothering to hide his contempt for Dexter's feigned ignorance regarding the availability of them. Dexter knew all about the young boys. Indeed. How clean they were, how beautiful, how well-endowed, how available—how cheap. Anyone who had read Burroughs knew about them. But he didn't need any young boy. He needed a carpet. That was all.

The craft cleared the harbor and picked up speed in the calm waters. He had little information about Morocco, having decided back in Chicago to visit only Spain and Portugal, despite Jean Paul's insistent letters and telephone calls that he should set aside time for *Tanger*. That's how he spelled it; as the Spanish did. "I promise you," he said, "after a few days with me, you'll want to move. Come to *Tanger*. This, darling, is the *city of broad shoulders*."

Dexter hadn't asked for advice, but Jean Paul offered it up just as he had when they'd lived together thirty years ago. As if they still lived together. And who was he to give advice? Imagine moving to Morocco and spending ones retirement chasing young Arab boys. What a ludicrous life. What about culture?

Jean Paul had mocked him: "You're retired and you live exactly as you have for the past forty years."

But he didn't; he didn't perform audits now. Besides, he'd seen his share of impoverished countries as an auditor—that's what made him uneasy. He'd tried every bookstore in Marbella and was unable to find a single brochure on Morocco—except for the Michelin guide in French—and simply wasn't prepared. After all Jean Paul couldn't be trusted for reliable information. So why was he going? Because he found Jean Paul amusing? He did. But, no. Definitely, no. He was going because he needed a carpet.

Across the aisle in the middle section were two American couples. The most vocal of the four tourists, a large woman with yellow hair, talked nonstop about food. "I'm going to have me some couscous," she said. "I love couscous." When the girl attendant walked past the seats with a small basket of hard, cellophane-wrapped candies, most everyone took a single piece, but the large woman fished out a handful, then looked at her friends and smiled. Dexter pulled off his glasses, slid them into their case. He removed the glossy magazine from the seat pocket and, after thumbing absently through it for a minute or two, he put his head back and fell asleep, and by the time he awoke they were entering the harbor at Tangier.

The city, a palette of pastels, spread out over the surrounding hills: a dramatic contrast to the pristine and homogeneous whitewashed Spain that Dexter had left behind one hour and a half earlier. Even at this distance there was the third-world promise of chipped paint and garbage-littered streets and ragged laundry strung on rooftop clotheslines. Still, compared to the boom of new, bad architecture that proliferated on the Costa del Sol, this place appeared at least to have been touched by the brush of creativity and originality.

The passengers were herding to the front by the entryway, and announcements were coming over the boat's intercom, alternating between Arabic and Spanish and English. Dexter could make no sense of the announcements; the English and Spanish were as garbled and unintelligible as the Arabic. The heavy, yellow-haired woman was urging her husband to be more aggressive: she waved her hand as if directing traffic, indicating that he should go to his left around a congested cluster of people then straight ahead along the left flank. "Carl, this isn't Magic Mountain," she yelled. "There aren't no lines."

The crew had set up a table at the portal inside the boat, and several local customs officials had come on board. None of them wore uniforms so it was difficult to discern the officials from others, who appeared only to be dockworkers of some kind. The windows were dirty, but Dexter could see well enough to know that a crowd had amassed outside.

"One day, one day," a man said, motioning people forward. Two officials, now seated behind the table, began to examine the passports thrust at them. Stamping, making notations on a sheet of paper, then handing them back. Dexter stayed at the rear of the mob; there was no need to rush. Why couldn't these people see that? There was no hurrying customs officials in these countries. The yellow-haired woman had managed to elbow her way to the front, having apparently given up on Carl, and when she submitted hers and her husband's passports and said something, the official put them in a wooden container the size of a shoe box. "Stand back, please," he said, his eyes fixed on some spot on the desk. "One day, one day," the first man said again. "Why don't we get *our* passports back?" the woman asked. The official did not acknowledge her and continued to stamp and return other people's documents. It was obvious to Dexter that whenever someone planned to stay longer than a day, his passport was put in the shoe box, but the woman apparently did not understand this and consulted nervously with her husband and the other couple.

Eventually the boat was emptied of one-day tourists, and the group of fifteen or twenty remaining people were allowed to go up the plank and onto the tarmac. Robed locals pressed forward, identifying themselves as guides; there were three or four to every visitor. There had still been no attempt to explain the delay in passport processing, even when the wooden box containing them was placed on the footpad of a moped and a boy rode off with it. One of the aggressive locals came close to Dexter, offering his services, dangling some sort of stamped, brass-colored medallion. He was younger than the others, with black, wavy hair and skin the color of coffee. Sticking out from his robe at the ankle were denim jeans, and he wore tennis shoes, not sandals. "Good morning; I am Joseph."

"Good morning, Joseph. I am Dexter Giles." He looked around the dock hoping to see Jean Paul, who had promised to meet him. There was another altercation between the woman and the senior official; he told her to go away and wait. "The passport will be returned after further investigation." He looked at her with such hatred that Dexter thought he might strike her to the concrete then swiftly kick her—he'd seen that once before the revolution in Iran—but nothing like that happened. She sat down on a pylon at the pier's edge and took a book out of her bag. *The Sheltering Sky*. One of the tour guides used this as an entree and began to tell the woman how Paul Bowles came to Tangier and thought it so beautiful that he decided to stay.

"You need a guide?" asked Joseph.

"I'm afraid not," said Dexter, looking around again.

The young man opened his palm to show his brass medallion. It was imprinted with a serial number. "I am official government guide for the tourists," he said. "Everything will be taken care of. Taxi, a good hotel, sightseeing, a tour through the marketplace."

"I've already made arrangements," said Dexter.

"Caves of Hercules, the Malcolm Forbes house, the King's winter palace. Would you like to ride a camel?"

"No." Dexter turned and walked away, over to the senior official. "How long are we going to be detained?"

There were few enough people now to enable Dexter to see that Jean Paul was not at the dock. Perhaps he was over by the taxis. But he said he had a car. "I'll pick you up in my gas-guzzler," he had said, reminding Dexter that the cost of gasoline was quite high in Morocco.

"You are perhaps waiting for someone?" The guide was hovering once again at Dexter's elbow.

"Yes."

"First trip to Tangier? You are American? I think you need a guide." He displayed his medallion again in his palm.

"Would you please wait until this passport business is concluded." Dexter raised his voice, and the young man retreated a few feet. Such reliance on a ridiculous piece of brass. Dexter's Abyssinians wore name tags that looked more official.

Dexter took his handkerchief from his pocket and blotted the perspiration from his forehead and temples. At last the boy on the moped returned with the wooden box, and the official began to distribute the passports. The blond woman closed her book and brushed off the seat of her shorts. Dexter accepted his passport and looked in the direction of the parked taxis, then the guide.

"I take you to a good hotel and later a tour. Yes?"

"How much?"

"Thirty-five dollars. Including everything."

"No. I don't want a tour." Dexter picked up his bag and started toward the line of taxis. The young man followed.

Dexter approached the pea-green Mercedes. The driver, positioned by his opened door, pulled open the door to the back seat. The young guide took Dexter's suitcase. "Take us to the Hotel Rembrandt," said the boy to the driver.

***

There were no draperies; the bed was in the midst of brilliant sunshine while the inside of the bathroom was so dark one could hardly expect a close shave. Technically, the room did have a view—the side of the building across the street—and if Dexter stuck his head out the window and craned to the left he could see the coastline, part of the beach, and the water. Was it the Mediterranean here or the Atlantic? Jean Paul had always been unreliable. Dexter remembered the time he'd been left to stand in the fumes and pollution at O'Hare after the long trip home from Milan.

He removed his glasses and rubbed his eyes, then took the slip of paper from his wallet and dialed Jean Paul's number. After three rings, his friend answered.

"You were supposed to meet me," said Dexter.

"I'll explain later," said Jean Paul. "Where are you?"

"Hotel Rembrandt. The lighting is *chiaroscuro*—I assume that explains the name."

Jean Paul chuckled. "Meet me at the Cafe de Paris. You're on the Boulevard Mohammed V. When you leave the hotel, turn right and walk up the boulevard for about ten minutes. It's on the right as you reach the roundabout. On the Place de France. You can't miss it."

The boulevard was Tangier's Fifth Avenue—crowded with shoppers and tourists—but the stores were basic: more like hardware stores than salons. Dexter stopped at a newsstand; all they had was yesterday's *Herald Tribune*, but he bought a copy anyway. This was a liberal Moslem country, so Jean Paul insisted, and Dexter did notice that not all the women were veiled, indeed some of the younger ones were dressed in western-style clothing as if they were employed by Price Waterhouse or Arthur Anderson. That was good. Dexter didn't have the strength or will to cope with a more radical political climate, as had been required during his years as an auditor. Jean Paul said that all Arabs hated

Westerners, and Dexter noticed that there were no book-stores with stacked copies of *The Satanic Verses* in the window.

He walked fast and avoided eye contact. That was the secret to avoid being hassled.

He found the cafe and glanced in through the open windows. Jean Paul wasn't inside. He took a seat at one of the outside tables and when the waiter appeared he ordered toast and coffee and began to read his paper. He became aware of the boy with the shoeshine kit standing behind the newspaper and when Dexter looked, the boy looked back, pleading and pointing to Dexter's shoes. What a face: features sharp and delicate, eyes clear and intelligent. Dexter's shoes were extremely dusty, so he nodded. And then he saw Jean Paul hurrying across the street.

"Desmonda, you look fantastic. You've lost weight." Jean Paul slapped him on the shoulder and squeezed in next to him, with his back to the restaurant and facing the street. He withdrew a cigarette, held the pack out to Dexter.

Dexter shook his head. "I joined a health club," he said. "And don't start with that *Desmonda* business."

"Pumping iron at your age?"

"Why didn't you meet me?"

"I was with the Marlboro man. He is so sexy; I've been trying to get that one for a year; I call him the Marlboro man because he sells cigarettes on the street corner."

***

Back in the room, Dexter lay on the bed to rest. The sun was low now, the noise from evening traffic more intense. The alienation he experienced was less from Tangier than Jean Paul, who'd always taken every opportunity to make fun of him. Why had he even asked him to visit? Of course, Dexter could answer the question: to show off his conquests like a pestiferous cat dragging a mouse into the house. The parade of swaggering young men past the cafe had surprised Dexter, though, and a great many of them had smiled at Jean Paul, knowingly, like secret lovers caught in a crowded elevator, and a few had even called out to him: "Hello, Jean Paul."

And Jean Paul sat there, proud as a father, nodding to this one and that one in his creased khakis and blue Lacoste polo with the collar turned up. And he was oh-so-knowledgeable, chastising Dexter because he overpaid the shoeshine boy and gave too generous a tip to the waiter. "I often spend the whole afternoon drinking tea and I know; ten dirhams is plenty," said Jean Paul. "You'll not survive in this town if you keep throwing your money around like that."

He waved and smiled, displaying his native cleverness. His head swiveled and bobbed, and after awhile Dexter found it impossible to take his eyes off the clumps of white hair, as coarse and stiff as bristles on a Cheshire hog, that sprouted from his friend's ears.

***

The clock over the reception desk showed the time as 9:25 A.M., but Dexter's watch was set at 9:20. He sat on in the lobby's only chair and unfolded his *Herald Tribune*, now two days old, and peeked at the hotel's entrance from behind the business section. He looked at the reception clock again and met the gaze of the clerk, who smiled.

And then at 9:30 he came through the door, confirming that Dexter's watch was set at the correct time and that Joseph was punctual—and a man of his word. "My friend," said Joseph, "good morning." Dexter rose and draped the camera over his shoulder, and the boy nodded. "That is good; there are many beautiful pictures in Tangier."

They stepped out into the sunshine where the taxi and driver from the day before waited at the curb. And after a slamming of doors the car rattled up the boulevard, past the Cafe de Paris, up into the surrounding hills. "Morocco is very liberal country," said the boy. "Moslems and Jews and Christians live together. We have no problems." The boy gestured with his brown, smooth hands; his fingers were slender and long and the nails were clean and neatly trimmed.

They entered a residential area of expensive houses and, at a bend in the road on top of the hill, Joseph pointed out King Hassan's winter palace; in Arabic he told the driver to stop and in English suggested that Dexter might want to take a picture of such a beautiful house. One saw finer estates on Chicago's Northshore, but Dexter focused and took several pictures from different angles, insisting that Joseph should be in at least one of the shots, and the boy stood in front of the gate as proudly as if it were the house of his own father.

And inside the caves there was a place where one could look out from the stalactites and dripping, calcareous dampness through an opening and onto the sea. It had something to do with Hercules. Joseph mentioned a legend of some kind but Dexter wasn't listening. He was noticing the boy's face, lit in the midst of darkness by the hole of light; he was looking at the straight, thin nose, the sharp chin, the full, dark lips, the hair thick and black, and eyes framed by lashes so thick, so heavy that he seemed unable to keep his eyes completely open. Dexter wanted to know if the boy came from the Atlas Mountains, if he was a Berber, but decided it would be improper to ask.

When they pulled off the dusty road to see the camels, Dexter was unyielding and obdurate—he would not care to ride a camel, thank you very much—until Joseph took off his robe and held it out to him. "Wear my jellaba; I will take a picture." The beast groaned and hissed with complaint as his owner prodded him to his feet and led him by the reins in a circle while Dexter teetered precariously on the strange saddle, barely able even for Joseph to manage a smile.

They went to the Medina and the Casbah and, when it was time for lunch, Dexter asked Joseph to join him so he wouldn't have to eat alone. They went to a restaurant crowded with, intended for, tourists on the second floor of a building. There were belly dancers and musicians, and people sat together at long, low tables all eating identical meals of tomato soup—which the waiter removed from the tray with his thumb submerged in the liquid—followed by lamb kabob and a flaky, spinach-filled pastry that Joseph called *pastella*. The yellow-haired woman was there with her husband and friends and she recognized Dexter and waved to him and he smiled and waved back. "We were here yesterday," she yelled across the room, over the hum of tourists and the noise of the tambourines. "Try the couscous. It's fantastic."

The food was average, but pleasurable because Joseph sat close on the banquette, explaining each course as carefully as if he were the elder and Dexter the child. When they went downstairs and into the street, the sun was hot and Dexter tried to stay in the shade, but the combination of food and heat made him wish for a moment to be back in his hotel, but then Joseph said he would take Dexter to see the Art College where students learned the ancient craft of weaving carpets. And Dexter had come to Tangier for the carpets, hadn't he?

The college was two flights up. The first floor, it appeared, was a leather store filled with racks of coats. Dexter paused for a moment to catch his breath and three salesmen approached and Dexter waved them away and forced himself to go on to the next floor. The room was large and open, filled with artisans and tourists, and stacked high with carpets. "I'll take you to the teacher," said Joseph, putting his hand on Dexter's arm and pulling him along. The floor was covered with new carpets of varying sizes and Dexter tried to step around them.

"Greetings, my friend," said the teacher—a large, bearded man with an enormous stomach that pushed out his robe so that the fabric gathered around his midsection causing the garment to ride higher in front than in back. He padded barefoot across the carpet quickly, his arms outstretched, to meet Dexter. "Welcome. Please, you must walk on the carpets. That is what they are for, my friend." He did a little dance, stomping up and down, to demonstrate. His feet were fat and flat, connected to thick, hairless ankles, and his toenails were yellow with patches of black fungus that ran all the way down to the cuticles. "Joseph," said the teacher, "take our friend to the roof and show him how we bake the carpets in the sun and when you return we will have tea. A very good, mint tea. Please." He motioned toward a door at the back of the room.

Dexter stepped onto the roof and leaned against the jamb of the door, just out of the sun. Joseph suggested another picture—the mosque in the distance was the oldest or the tallest or the most beautiful—and Dexter handed him the camera without speaking.

Then he trudged down the steps and over to the wall and slumped on the bench that ran the length of it. The teacher clapped his hands twice and an assistant, or student, appeared with a tall, clear glass of tea. "Hold it like this," said the teacher, and he demonstrated by gripping the top and bottom edges with his thumb and forefinger. "This way you will not get burned." There were green soggy leaves floating on top like seaweed and the tea was far too sweet for Dexter's taste, but he was tired and thankful for the chance to sit and rest. But then, like a colony of ants, boys began to carry carpets to him, depositing them eagerly at his feet. "If you choose the most beautiful carpet, which color would it be?" said the teacher.

"Well—"

"This green one, or this blue? Maybe you like red. I think you like this red one." The carpets kept coming, piled now as high as Dexter's knees.

"Do you have runners?" asked Dexter.

"My friend, we have everything. Which is your very favorite of these?"

"I don't really need this size. But the green is a nice color."

Two claps. "Take these away. Leave the green and the blue." Carpet runners began to appear on the stack. Boys hurried in and out bringing ones of all colors and lengths, and the teacher swirled and darted like a boxer, psyched and fresh, as if at the start of round one.

Joseph sat next to Dexter. "Are these not beautiful carpets?" he said, speaking confidentially into Dexter's ear.

"How is your tea?" said the teacher. "Would you like a cigarette?" He lit one and immediately dropped it on the top carpet. "See, you cannot hurt these carpets. Very strong. Which carpet do you like?"

"Well—"

"Which do you like?"

"I—"

"This one or this one?"

"The red with the hieroglyphics is—"

"How much do you think for this carpet?"

"I really—"

"Would you believe two thousand dollars only for this beautiful carpet?" The teacher was stooped and close, peering into Dexter's eyes.

"Two thousand dollars?" said Dexter, now very much awake. "I think not."

The teacher gave him a look of disgust and stomped away, but when Dexter started to rise, he wheeled around and strode back, a Welcome-to-Cartier smile smeared across his face.

"I'm afraid my budget—"

"You have American Express?" He was close again, his eyes like two gold coins. "You don't have to pay." He laughed. "Put it on the credit card."

"No, two thousand—"

"What is the most you are willing to pay for this most beautiful carpet? How much?" He placed his hands on Dexter's shoulders and leaned in, and Joseph rested his forehead against Dexter, just above the ear. The boy's hair was soft; he smelled sweet and nutty, like almonds. Joseph whispered in his ear. "It is beautiful, yes?"

***

Jean Paul was looking down into the Casbah from his terrace. Dexter was stretched out on a chaise. "And that was Barbara Hutton's house. She lived there with her gorgeous bullfighter with the tremendous cock."

Dexter yawned.

"Desmonda, get up. You must see this boy. Oh, look at his bow legs. He is so sexy. He was in prison; he killed someone. But I like him. I think he's sexy."

Dexter stood and went over to the edge and placed his hands on top of the ledge. "That one?" He pointed. "You think he's sexy? You've been away too long."

Jean Paul's head snapped around and he eyed Dexter for a moment. "What's that supposed to mean? You don't think he's sexy? Or are you pretending you wouldn't like to meet a boy?"

"I've already met a young man," said Dexter.

"Who? I know everyone here."

Dexter went back to the chaise and lay back and folded his hands in his lap. "You don't know this one. I asked."

"What's his name?"

"Can I get you more coffee?" Dexter leaned forward and held up his cup. Jean Paul followed him closely down the narrow, tiled stairway and into the kitchen, asking why Dexter was being so secretive, so coy, asking why Dexter had decided to stay on at the Rembrandt; then he followed him back up the stairs, interrogating and petulant, and onto the roof again.

"His name is Joseph," said Dexter.

That was all it took. Jean Paul was relentless. *Joseph* was a common name—not as common as *Mohammed*—but common. At first it was fun teasing Jean Paul, but knowing the boy's name was like a taste of blood, and Dexter soon regretted having said anything.

It was the same as years before in Chicago. When Jean Paul lost his job at the Hilton, Dexter had taken him in, allowed him to use the spare bedroom. But when Dexter left for Milan—an assignment that kept him away for over six weeks—Jean Paul had taken too quickly to his hospitality while he searched, at a leisured pace, for a new position. He made use of the kitchen, the phone, the car, and found his way eventually into Dexter's larger and brighter bedroom. There was one snag, of course. The snag's name being *Russell*.

Dexter turned away from Jean Paul and looked down into the Casbah. A new group of tourists were getting the one-day hustle; their guide pointed up, to the top of the wall and the terrace where he and Jean Paul stood. He remembered the spiel: "This is the old section, but there are many wealthy people."

There were buildings on three sides of the Casbah, and on the fourth side, to the right, an ancient wall with an arched doorway that afforded access to the sea. Through the keyhole opening the water shimmered, brilliant and blue. As soon as Dexter met someone, Jean Paul had to meet them—he had to have sex with them too, and then make sure that Dexter found out. Jean Paul narrowed it down to five Josephs, then to four, then three, then two—both *official* government tour guides. "One has a brown mole below his navel," said Jean Paul. "Does he have a mole?" He pulled down the elastic band of his khaki trousers and indicated the position. "Here, on his right side."

"I didn't say I slept with him," said Dexter. "He helped me choose a carpet. He likes me. He's taking me sightseeing again tomorrow."

Jean Paul fell into the chair next to Dexter, snorting with derisive laughter. "He doesn't like you. These people don't like anyone. They only want your money."

***

The tours of the Medina and the Casbah and the camel rides were tourist attractions. Nothing more. Dexter might as well have chosen Los Angeles, with its theme parks and movie studios and tours of celebrities' homes, for his holiday. One did not really understand a place or its people by observing the veneer.

And so: while the seeming familiarity of this restaurant, located a block off the Boulevard Mohammed on an upwardly sloping street, comforted Dexter it also stimulated him with the prospect of discovery. The square, Formica-covered tables, the wooden, straight-backed chairs, and the refrigerated deli case were fixtures that would be found in any small town or suburb at home. And while the name, *Tony's*, and the food, Italian, of course, had initially come as a surprise to him, Dexter realized now, that it was precisely because the high-ceilinged room was large and square and absent of decor or anything but utilitarian lighting that people came. They came for the food.

Because only when one understood the similarities could one appreciate the differences.

Joseph sat across from him, wearing Levis and a starched cotton shirt; attire that contributed to the sense of something already seen that Dexter was experiencing. Their table, wedged against a column and under stairs which led to a rest room and the balcony with additional tables for dining was, given the overall lack of atmosphere in the restaurant, one of the better tables and actually afforded a certain degree of privacy.

Not that Joseph had ever appeared messy, but there was something about him—he had shaved and combed his hair—that made Dexter think he had taken a little extra time to get ready for their dinner. That Joseph had discarded his jellaba for western-style clothing pleased Dexter. He was a great believer in symbolism.

Joseph took intermittent bites of spaghetti, pausing briefly between to tell Dexter about Marrakech, dimples flickering at the sides of his mouth as he spoke.

"I can take you," he said.

"How much commission did you make on the rug?" said Dexter. The boy did not stop chewing, but slowed a bit. "Joseph, it doesn't have to be a secret. You're entitled to a commission. I wanted a carpet."

The boy finished his food, took a pack of cigarettes from his shirt pocket, and offered one to him. Dexter started to refuse then accepted and allowed Joseph to light it for him. His hands and nails were so smooth and immaculately shaped that Dexter couldn't help but imagine how they might feel against his cheek.

He blinked twice, to lubricate his new, bifocal contact lenses, and looked around the room, glancing up at the tables on the balcony. There was the one aspect to remind him of his presence in an Arab country. The restaurant was solely inhabited by men; there wasn't one woman in the place—not at the tables, not behind the deli case, not in the kitchen. He wondered if the yellow-haired woman had noticed the boys. Perhaps back at home she had a son or even two, maybe even Joseph's age. He pictured her issuing orders to her husband back on the boat. He imagined her at home back in the States in a cheaply-built tract house making all the decisions. Deciding what everyone would have for dinner; choosing the movies and the television shows; deciding what kind of van the family would buy; deciding what breed of dog the children would have and then picking its name. No doubt it had even been her idea to come to Morocco in the first place. And where was she now? Rushing in and out of stores with Carl in tow? Or back at the tourist restaurant with its belly dancers and Moroccan orchestra?

"Marrakech is very different," said Joseph. "Beautiful mountains, beautiful flowers, beautiful sun."

"No more shopping. I don't want to buy anything else," said Dexter.

"You will rest in the sun. I will take very good care of you," said Joseph.

***

Dexter spotted the yellow-haired woman the minute he stepped on board the boat. She waved; Dexter waved back and smiled, then headed for the upper deck. Perhaps she and her husband and the other couple had gone to Marrakech as well. He hadn't seen her though—but then he hadn't even ventured from the hotel for the entire three days, being content to relax by the pool and take his meals in his room with Joseph.

He settled in a seat near the back and placed the bag with his carpet in the adjoining seat. It was folded in half, rolled tight, and tied with twine.

There were no less than half a dozen messages from Jean Paul when Dexter checked back into the Rembrandt. "I knew you hadn't left the country," he said. "I checked with my sources." And then, on his last day, Jean Paul had practically dragged him through the maze of narrow, sunless passageways to the shops. "There would be no point in trying to return it," he said, turning his head for a moment to speak. His bony elbows seesawed through the air as he rushed along. In the shops he pointed to carpets hanging on the walls and stacked in the corners. "See," he said, "and most are less than a hundred dollars."

In the last store Dexter walked over to one of the stacks. "My carpet is much larger and it's an irregular size," said Dexter. He lifted up a corner. "Mine is more detailed than these—and the weave is tighter."

"Well you paid a thousand dollars," said Jean Paul.

"Eight hundred and fifty," said Dexter.

"You got screwed. Your precious little Joseph is on commission. You should have your head examined throwing money at him like that. You're the biggest fish he ever caught."

"You've never been with Joseph, have you?" said Dexter.

Jean Paul turned away and pointed to the brass sconces in the corner of the room, shaped like hooded cobras, intended for candles.

"Choose a restaurant," said Dexter. "I'll take you to dinner. Who knows if we'll see each other again."

The boat was moving fast now; he took a last look at Tangier. He glanced at the carpet, ran his hand across the exposed surface to feel the weave. He remembered Joseph's face and hair, saw the dimples at the corners of his mouth, but even now the boy's features were fading, like a photograph exposed to the Sahara sun. The memory of his farewell embrace, though, back in the room at the Rembrandt would live for as long as the carpet. All Dexter had to do was look at the runner and touch it; all he had to do was to run his hand over it to see the slope of Joseph's shoulders and his smooth, bare chest and his flat stomach and the trace of light hair that ran down from his navel; all he had to do was touch it to see the small, brown mole on the left and at the top of the vee where his torso joined with his long, brown legs.

The Earl

The pot roast was gone. And so too: the skinless chicken breasts and the leg of lamb and the boneless pork loin and the frozen turkey and the package of veal chops and the sirloin steaks and the corned beef and the picnic ham. The only items left were the two TV dinners, one roasting chicken with freezer burn, a package of frozen bagels, and two unwrapped pork chops which would soon be as white and tasteless as dry ice. Dexter stood in front of the refrigerator, arms akimbo, tapping his foot on the linoleum floor. Had the man entertained an entire company of new recruits from the Great Lakes Naval Training Center? Dexter stepped into the pantry, took a glance at the shelves, made a visual inventory: there were no soft drinks left, most of the wine was gone, and the bottle of Crown Royal was empty. Why had he even bothered to put it back? Dexter returned to the refrigerator, pulled open the freezer door for a second look. Even the ice trays were empty, though Jean Paul had installed a new bottle of vodka, a cheap brand with the design of a black and red eagle on the label.

In the living room, Dexter picked up a pair of dirty blue jeans and a flannel shirt and scuffed cowboy boots and took them to the closet in the front hall. The whole house smelled of stale cigarette smoke. He couldn't wait to see this one. Not that he needed to. He could picture the waif: mousy brown hair, the beginning of a moustache, prickly chin, acne, unkempt fingernails, white skin, sunken chest, legs bowed from a childhood of poor nutrition, and—given Jean Paul's sexual proclivities—a large penis.

Debit and Credit rubbed against Dexter's leg when he flushed the toilet in the downstairs bathroom. Jean Paul claimed to like animals, but his affection apparently stopped short of cleaning the litter box: from the smell, and the weight, it hadn't been changed once in the four weeks that Dexter had been gone.

He picked up the cats, carried them to the kitchen, and put them down. He stared at the dirty dishes in the sink, then rinsed out a dry, dusty pet bowl, filled it with water, and set it back on the floor. As Dexter opened the can of chicken—with real chunks of cheese—and filled the two monogrammed bowls, Debit and Credit stood on hind legs, purring loudly. It did smell good; it's a wonder Jean Paul hadn't eaten it as well.

Dexter carried his suitcases into his room and put them on the bed. The spread was wrinkled, the pillows flat, as if the bed had been used and hastily remade. And then before he could stop himself Dexter had stomped down the hall to the guest bedroom and was pounding hard on the door with his knuckled fist.

"Jean Paul, you were supposed to pick me up at the airport. Get your boney ass out of there. We need to talk."

No response. Dexter opened his mouth, started to yell at the door again, but did not. He hadn't slept on the trip home. His back was already stiff and sore from the packed flight, and his jaw had started to hurt from gritting his teeth. He reached for the knob and twisted. The door had been locked from the inside.

He walked back down the hall to the front bedroom. He sat on the edge of his bed, opened and closed his mouth, contracted and expanded his fingers, in an effort to reduce stress. He stood and pulled back the spread and top sheet, then he removed his glasses and put his face close. The bottom, fitted sheet was wrinkled and soiled with grease spots. Dexter plucked a brown, curly hair from the pillow and held it up to the light.

***

He folded the last pair of socks and placed them in the wicker basket. Debit had settled in the middle of the freshly laundered and folded sheets and was licking his paw. Dexter shut the dryer, closed the concealing louver doors—leaving a crack for Debit to get out—and went over to the galley area of his kitchen for a second cup of coffee. This was his favorite part of the house with its restaurant range and glass-fronted refrigerator-freezer unit, and ordinarily he enjoyed spending time here—especially upon his return from an extended, overseas audit—and he even felt a momentary pulse of joy when the announcer stated that Brahms's D Major Concerto for Violin and Orchestra would follow, after a short intermission for the headlines, until he spotted the dead African violets in the window and remembered Jean Paul, sequestered away in the upstairs bedroom. This caused him to abruptly pound his fist, once, on the countertop. Credit, who had been winding around and between his legs, dashed away in a straight line, her tail held stiff and high. She hesitated at the edge of the kitchen, turned, and looked back at Dexter; when apparently satisfied that she was in no danger, she slowly made her way back to rub at his ankles once again.

At the kitchen table, Dexter gazed out over the back patio. It was time for spring planting; perhaps he'd go to the nursery on Saturday. He opened his briefcase, took out his expense account form and the envelope of receipts, and was converting the lire on the hotel bill to dollars when he heard a cough and looked up. The boy stood in the kitchen doorway wearing nothing but white tube socks and a pair of blue, cotton jockey shorts with a white waistband.

"I'm Russell," he said, yawning and reaching down to take hold of his crotch, "from Tennessee. Anymore of that coffee? I got a real sucker of a hangover."

Dexter turned away, pretended to be studying the papers spread out on the table. The boy's beauty surprised and embarrassed him. Why the kid was positively angelic-looking, almost cherubic: he had an adolescent yet muscular physique, smooth, hairless skin, and that face. My God, that face. The square jaw, the delicate nose, the cleft chin, the dimpled smile, the blue eyes—so large, so expressive, so *simpatico*—and the wheat-colored curls crowning his head, with that one soft loop that dangled out over his forehead. In khaki slacks and a blazer he could stroll the campus at Exeter; a face such as this could grace the cover of *Teen*; put a tennis racquet in his hand and you could take him anywhere.

The boy—Russell—came into the center of the kitchen and picked up Credit. He cradled her in his right arm and scratched under her chin with his left hand. "What kind of cats are these?"

"She seems to like you," said Dexter. He stood, and looking down at the floor, brushed past Russell on his way to the coffee pot. "Abyssinians."

"I don't take no sugar or cream," said Russell. "Make it hot and black, like my—"

"Would you like some supper? I'm afraid the larder is rather bare, but I could make you some tuna salad." Dexter peered over the top of his reading glasses.

Russell grinned and nodded and went over to the window. He sat at the table and Debit jumped up into his lap. Dexter took down the can of tuna and gathered the celery seed and dried parsley and garlic powder and put the eggs on to boil; he didn't like using dried ingredients but there was nothing fresh left. When he opened the can of tuna, Debit and Credit gathered at this feet—and as he mixed the hard boiled eggs and mayonnaise and seasonings, Russell got up and came over also. The boy hadn't said much; he seemed content to stare out the window, though he had broken the silence to tell Dexter that he thought his house was real beautiful and to ask what kind of car Dexter drove. Nor did he seem to mind standing around in his underwear or being looked at. But Dexter didn't stare. When he turned and reached for plates, he felt a hand on the middle of his back.

"It looks real good," said Russell. "Much oblige."

Dexter put his papers in the briefcase, set it on the floor away from the table, then brought the sandwiches over.

"What kind of bread is this?" said Russell.

"It's a toasted poppy seed bagel," said Dexter.

Russell made an approving *umm* sound and finished the sandwich in three bites. He smiled at Dexter; mayonnaise smeared his lips and gathered at the corners of his mouth like spittle. For a moment Dexter considered taking a tissue and moistening it with his saliva to wipe the boy's face clean—like one of those mothers who behaves as if she and her child still share the same bodily fluids.

"Do you always eat so fast?" said Dexter.

"I started working out—at the 'Y.' I've already put on some bulk." Russell flexed his pectoral muscles and thumped his chest with his fist. "Feel," he said.

Dexter reached out.

"Desmonda, you're home," said Jean Paul, from the doorway. "How was Italy?" Dexter jerked back his hand and picked up his napkin and wiped his own mouth. He sat quietly and took several deep breaths before standing to clear the table. He walked to the sink with his arms full.

Jean Paul leaned against the door jamb like one of those middle-aged male models: smirking, in his bare feet, left foot on top of the right, and oh-so-comfortable with his hands shoved in the front pockets of the robe. Dexter's robe. Dexter's new, hooded, white terry cloth robe with the square pockets and navy trim. Dexter looked away and began to rinse the plates at the sink. "Did you find a job?" he said.

"Well it's nice to see you too. I see you've met Russell."

"This is not a hotel. You can't stay here forever."

"How do you like that, Russell?" said Jean Paul. "Not even a thank you for looking after his precious cats."

Less than six feet away, on the window sill, sat the withered violets. "Of course," said Dexter. "The cats demanded so much of your time you didn't have an opportunity to water the plants. Yes, of course, that makes perfect sense."

"You guys sound like my mother and her boyfriend," said Russell. "She and Dwayne fight like mountain lions."

***

Dexter crouched at the edge of the brick patio, surrounded by flats of geraniums and petunias and impatiens and clay pots. He left the back door open so that he could hear the stereo, listening for the second time this morning to a recording of *Carmina Burana* by Carl Orff, having purposely adjusted the bass so that the windows rattled. A few months earlier he played the music for Jean Paul, who said after listening for only a few minutes, that the piece was too bombastic, too avant garde; he preferred instead the music of Elgar and Sibelius. This morning, the first time, Dexter put the *Carmina Burana* on a little before seven. Rise and shine Jean Paul: here's your morning wake up call. Less than twenty minutes later, with the walls oscillating from the chorus's roaring and the floors undulating from the percussion, Jean Paul charged out the front door and flounced down the front steps like a diva who has been told that her rendition of the opera's defining aria lacks spirit. Dexter had smiled and turned the volume higher: it was his house; he'd do as he pleased.

He dropped a mixture of compost and cow manure in the pot and removed a large, red geranium from its plastic container and placed it in the center of one of the larger pots. This color, a candy-apple red, simply shrieked drama. These days there was such a wide range of color and variety available; when he was a boy there was just that one dull shade of red with velvety leaves. Dexter broke off a leaf and held it under his nose. He had always preferred the organic, earthy smell of geraniums and chrysanthemums and daisies to the heavy, perfumed smell of lilies or myrtle or magnolias.

Last night after Russell left the house, Dexter had gone to bed. Despite the jet lag, or perhaps because of it, he'd been slow to fall asleep. He simply couldn't chase the image of that face. He awoke at two-thirty and at three and again at four, the boy's lips and arms and small round nipples roiled in his head, an absurd collage, troubling his sleep, disquieting his brain. It was a foolish and unreasonable obsession; there was simply no recompense for such thoughts. The ache of unrequited love was undeniable. But for a nineteen-year-old, uneducated boy from the rural south, a boy nearly thirty years his junior, a boy young enough to be his son, a boy young enough to be his grandson—a boy whose own father would think Dexter old.

Dexter, still crouched on his knees, dropped his head and closed his eyes.

"Those are beautiful flowers," said the boy. "You've got a real fancy yard here." Dexter raised his head, opened his eyes.

"Russell" he said. He took off his gloves, dropped them to the bricks, and stood. His joints popped; his ankles creaked. He extended his hand. "It's good to see you, but I'm afraid Jean Paul is not here—he had errands, I believe."

Russell hesitated, then stuck out his hand too, but he didn't squeeze back when Dexter tightened his grasp; his arm and hand remained limp and lifeless. "That don't matter," said Russell. "I like you."

Dexter cleared his throat and swallowed. "You have large, well-shaped hands. You must develop a proper handshake," he said, reaching for Russell's hand again. "When I squeeze, squeeze back. Like this."

The boy widened his eyes and stared at Dexter, as if unable to interpret this unexpected—and uncustomary?—interest in him. Had he been boxed about by an abusive father to such an extent that he could not distinguish between constructive, well-intentioned criticism and that designed to degrade and demoralize? But, now, Dexter knew he was getting ahead of himself. He had no information to support his sudden hypothesis that Russell had been mistreated or otherwise abused—in a physical or verbal sense. Russell bit the inside of his cheek, tightened his grip, and when Dexter smiled, he smiled back.

Russell wore the same boots, overrun at the heels, and the same jeans that he had worn when he left Dexter's house some twelve hours earlier, but he had on a different shirt—a polyester, long-sleeved, flowered print with the first three buttons undone, which caused or allowed the material to gape open and ride back on his shoulders, exposing the left side of his chest and a crescent of pink areola and nipple.

***

Only after Graciela scrubbed and swabbed and swept for eight uninterrupted hours on Monday, only when the kitchen appliances glistened and the bathrooms sparkled and the tabletops reflected like mirrors did Dexter feel that he had regained any semblance of control in his life. He entered the living room, scanned left and right, up and down. The oversized, square pillows had been pummeled and pounded and thrashed, then placed back on the couch so that they stood at attention like plump soldiers. Dexter settled in the wing back chair, flanking the fireplace, that afforded the view through the bay window to the front steps. Midway through the April issue of *Architectural Digest*, he came to a series of pictures that featured an estate on the Mediterranean. The villa had a kidney-shaped swimming pool surrounded by lush vegetation overlooking the sea; stone steps terraced down from the gardens to the water. Dexter closed his eyes, imagined himself sitting in a chaise at the pool's edge and watching as Russell walked toward him in skimpy, red tank trunks, his hairless body bronzed and slick and fragrant with a patina of coconut-scented oil.

And then the heavy oak and glass front door slammed shut and Dexter opened his eyes. Jean Paul strode across the room and slumped in the wing back opposite, clutching a pack of unfiltered cigarettes in his hand. He held them out, and Dexter extracted one, put it in his mouth, and stretched to reach the flame of his friend's thin, gold lighter. Jean Paul leaned back in a cloud of smoke and sighed dramatically.

"So, what happened with the position at the Marriott?" said Dexter.

"They wanted a desk clerk," said Jean Paul.

"And the Fremont?"

"It's a third-rate chain."

Dexter laid the cigarette in the ashtray and walked slowly into the dining room, where he poured two glasses of whiskey from a crystal decanter. On the way back to his chair he set one of the glasses on Jean Paul's end table.

"You may have to swallow your pride," said Dexter, swallowing a mouthful of whiskey.

"I'm Swiss-trained; I don't intend to schlepp around in some fleabag *pensione* in an ill-fitting uniform."

"Well, after what happened at the Hilton."

Jean Paul inhaled deeply and stubbed out the cigarette. Gripping the arms of the chair, as if suddenly fearful that he might be asked to give up his seat, he squinted at Dexter and said in a growl: "I've written to Eugenia in Bern—"

"You live in the United States now. Nobody here cares about deposed European royalty—"

"Oh really? And that's why Nixon put the White House guards in Prussian military uniforms? That's why everyone is so interested in Princess Grace? I was Eugenia's guest at her villa in Lago Lugano. She *is* a Romanoff. Her father knows people in the hotel industry. Just because you're content to carry your own luggage and travel in tourist class on ten hour flights with that steamer trunk you call a briefcase—"

"It's an audit bag and I don't have to travel tourist class." Dexter sipped his whiskey, forced a smile. "If I choose to save the company money by—"

"Ha. Choose? Do you think your precious chairman flies tourist? Do you think the chairman of Imperial Petroleum would stoop to fly commercial? You with your misguided loyalty. You're pathetic."

"At least I have a position. And I have a house and a car and I have been more than generous in allowing you to stay here and abuse my good intentions while you get on your feet. You're quite the grandame on other peoples' money."

"Without me you would never meet anyone like Russell. Face it, Desmonda, you have no life; you have no friends. You're damned fortunate to have me here."

Dexter and Jean Paul had gradually sat forward in their chairs until their faces were just a few feet apart. Jean Paul glanced at this watch, then sat back. "Did Russell come by?"

Dexter leaned back too. "Stop calling me Desmonda. I told you I don't think it's funny. And I have enough conflict at work; I don't appreciate coming home to more of the same."

***

Tuesday had been set aside for personal business trips: to the dry cleaner, to the bank, to the veterinarian. In the afternoon he'd relax, listen to some music, read, have supper, and get to bed early: Wednesday he was due back in the office. It promised to be a long day, with the door closed and him drafting the audit report. By week's end the new schedule would be out. There'd been talk of sending him to Pakistan. Two months in a country where liquor was banned, two months in a country so violent that an armor-plated car had to be used to transport Imperial personnel to and from the office, two months in a country so radical that the auditors had to live within a walled compound, two months in fact of virtual imprisonment. If he could only be scheduled for Trinidad or Venezuela or even Argentina, he could stop off on the way for a week of vacation in Puerto Rico or the Virgin Islands.

How much fun it would be to take Russell for a week of Caribbean sun and relaxation.

Dexter carried the dry cleaning and his briefcase to the back porch and set them down and went back into the house to get Debit and Credit, already installed in the kennel carrier. Dexter put his index finger in one of the holes of the wire grating and felt Debit's cold, wet nose. The cat let out a mournful, wailing meow and rubbed his whiskers against Dexter's finger. He put the case down and locked the door, then picked it up again and descended the steps to the yard. The sun was shining rather intensely for late April. Dexter checked his newly-planted pots and made a mental note to water them in the afternoon after he had completed his errands. It took two trips to carry the cats and the laundry and the briefcase across the patio to the garage, and it was when he looked up with his key to unlock the garage door that he saw Russell in the alley peering through the iron fence into the yard.

"I figured you might be planting more flowers," said the boy, "and I reckoned you'd need help."

Russell wore different jeans—powder-blue and quite tight with the top button unfastened—and no shirt. It was stuffed in a hip pocket so that it hung down and swung freely when he walked.

Dexter glanced over his shoulder and up at the second floor window where Jean Paul slept, then back at Russell. "I have errands, but you could come with me—if you'd like." Dexter reached inside and pressed the button to activate the garage door opener. Russell stooped and entered from the back before the door was all the way open and looked around.

"Cool car," said Russell.

"BMW: Bavaria," said Dexter.

"Cool," said Russell.

Driving down Clark Street, some twenty or thirty blocks from the Loop, Dexter momentarily regretted having asked Russell along. There was always the possibility of running into someone from the office, though he thought it unlikely on a Tuesday. Still, with the sun shining so brightly, with the windows open and the sunroof back, with Russell sitting next to him bare-chested: this would be difficult to explain. It was bad enough with strangers, though no one looked askance or suggested anything untoward when Russell followed close behind him at the cleaners, or when he tagged along as he dropped off Debit and Credit at the veterinarians. Russell started to come inside at the bank too, but Dexter asked him to keep an eye on the car, feigning concern that someone might back into it or open their door, dinging the chrome.

When Dexter returned, Russell was sitting on the driver's side, his right hand on the wheel, his left arm resting on the door. Dexter put on his prescription sunglasses and reached for the door handle.

"Mind if I give her a spin?" said Russell. He smiled and before Dexter could respond he had jumped from the car and taken Dexter by the arm. "Man like you needs a chauffeur," he said. And Dexter allowed himself to be led around the back to the other side. Russell pulled open the door and bowed from the waist. "Where to, Mister—" He paused. "I don't know your last name," he said.

"Giles," said Dexter, climbing into the passenger seat. "I'm not sure about the uniform, Russell."

"You want I should take my pants off?" Russell winked and closed the door. He slapped Dexter on the shoulder. "Cause I will if that's what you want. My girlfriend says I'm a crazy man."

Russell got in behind the wheel and started the engine and turned to Dexter. "Where to, boss?"

Lunch? He could take the boy to lunch, but where could they go with him wearing so little. "Are you hungry?"

"Let's go to The Earl," said Russell, "and have a drink." He put the car in gear, backed out of the space, and drove to the street entrance. He pulled out, made an immediate left onto Broadway, headed south at a fast clip. Dexter fastened his seat belt.

Russell pulled into a narrow alley, full of potholes and litter, drove about half a block, and stopped. When he began to back up next to a brick building, Dexter said: "You're not parking here?"

"We can go in the back way," said Russell. "There." He pointed through the windshield, to a half flight of steps just ahead that led up to a blackened, wooden door.

"No," said Dexter. "We'll park in a lot or a garage."

"Trust me," said Russell.

Dexter started to say that he didn't use back entrances—and that he didn't park in alleys—but seeing as how it was the middle of the day, and since Russell was dressed so casually, perhaps it would be all right this one time to make an exception.

He followed the boy to the stairs. Russell stopped on the landing at the top and held open the door, and Dexter stepped out of the sunlight and into a dimly-lit and disordered kitchen which also functioned as a storage room: industrial shelving held cartons of supplies; cases of beer and liquor and soda were stacked against bare walls and in the open areas of the room. Russell gestured for him to go on ahead, and Dexter followed the path among the boxes to the front of the room and a swinging door with porthole. The aroma of cheap pipe tobacco lingered in the second room, but it was somewhat brighter and smelled less sour than the kitchen had with its cases of empties and soiled bar rags strewn about.

The Earl, occupying two floors of an old brownstone in the near north section of the city, was one of Chicago's oldest gay bars; there were of course other hustler bars in the city, but management here had grand aspirations, having chosen what was once a beautiful old mansion from the turn of the century for their establishment. These days the place had the ambiance of a bordello. Jean Paul frequented the bar with regularity and had brought Dexter here on two or three occasions in the past. The former front parlour, an entertainment room with cushioned settees upholstered in red to match the flocked, red wallpaper, featured cabaret acts: one evening Dexter heard a diminutive older man, who referred to himself as a song stylist, deliver—in a whine and a lisp—the usual and expected renditions of "I Did It My Way" and "I Gotta Be Me" and "People, People Who Need People." All of the numbers were delivered with vibrato and panache, if not arresting talent—he didn't tickle the ivories; he beat them into submission with fat, bejeweled fingers—but today the parlour was empty. The middle room, with its horseshoe-shaped bar, contained what little action there was at The Earl on this particular afternoon. Two men, on opposite sides of the bar and apparently alone, stared past each other into space, or perhaps at the series of framed prints which featured mounted horses, their riders in formal hunting gear, jumping vine-covered walls and bushes in pursuit of a fox. Walnut woodwork and bar stools, upholstered in green leather and secured with brass studs, completed the exclusive-men's-club look. At the far end of the room a dark, slender boy with shoulder-length, curly hair and a moustache stood next to—leaned against—a heavy man, perhaps Dexter's age. The man's round, red face was framed by a full head of silver hair that accentuated the ruddy hue of his complexion, and his fat legs hung over his bar stool like a stack of waffles.

Russell had taken a look in the other room, then come back to take a stool, patting the one adjacent, nodding at Dexter. The bartender, a sallow-complexioned man, approached from the cash register, located at the open end of the horseshoe, and after giving Dexter a quick, vaguely inquisitive look, directed his attention to the boy.

"You have to have a shirt on, Russell," he said.

"No problem, Ed," said Russell. He pulled the shirt out of his hip pocket, held it up in his fist a few inches from the man's face. "I got a shirt, Ed," he said.

"I don't want no trouble today, Russell."

"Hey, Ed, no trouble. Me and Mr. Giles want a drink, that's all." The boy's jaw tensed, his eyes were large and unflinching.

"What's it going to be?" said the man, pressing cocktail napkins to the lacquered surface.

Russell ordered a rum and Coke, then looked at Dexter and flashed a toothsome smile. Dexter asked for a negroni.

When the bartender put down the drinks, Russell asked Dexter if he had a buck for cigarettes and without waiting for an answer asked the bartender, Ed, for change. The boy hopped off his stool with the quarters, circled the bar, and jaunted through the doorway to the hallway; he had a way of walking, landing lightly on the heels, raising up onto the balls of the feet, that seemed peculiar and common to boys from the country. In an alcove, under the staircase, Dexter watched as he fed coins into the machine. The two men who had stared into space watched as well; one had turned completely around on his stool as Russell pulled the handle and stooped to retrieve the pack from the tray. Russell turned, stripped off the cellophane band, peeled back the foil, and tamped the pack hard against his palm, then withdrew a cigarette and lit it before reëntering the room. He went around the other end of the bar to make a selection on the jukebox, cigarette dangling from his lips, then stopped to exchange words with the red-faced man and curly-headed boy.

After a brief conversation he came over and sat back down next to Dexter. "How are we doing?" he said. The volume of the music was turned high, no doubt to compensate for a more crowded room, and Dexter recognized the boy's selection as a current hit entitled: "Disco Inferno." "You dig The Tramps?" said Russell. Dexter nodded and smiled. Russell knocked back the rest of his drink and held up his glass and yelled: "Hey, Ed, how about another round?" Ed looked at Dexter and when he held up two fingers the man began to make the drinks.

Russell put the pack of cigarettes and the book of matches on the bar. Dexter picked up the matches. The outside cover had a sketch of an old English pub with a sign identifying it as The Earl; the inside had a place to write one's name and telephone number with a caption that read: *We met at The Earl.* Dexter lit a cigarette and took a sip of his negroni.

"You got any kids?" said Russell.

"Me?" said Dexter. "No, no kids."

"Was you ever married?"

"Married? No, I've never been married."

"Don't like pussy, huh?"

"Not especially," said Dexter.

"I love pussy," said Russell.

"I have to go to the men's room," said Dexter.

"I miss you already," said Russell. He smiled and emptied his glass with a large swallow. "Okay if I get another?"

Dexter nodded. "But none for me."

He made his way to the doorway, turned right at the cigarette machine, and walked down the hallway to the door with the silhouette of a man in riding attire. He shivered as he began to urinate in a full, heavy stream; he wondered now what Jean Paul and Russell had done sexually—and if the boy had been a willing partner.

When he got back to the bar, Russell had already finished half of his new drink and had ordered another one for him.

"Is this where you met Jean Paul?" said Dexter.

"I've seen him here," said the boy.

Dexter moved his head in a circular motion to relieve the stiffness in his neck; there was something about sitting on a bar stool—any stool for that matter—that threw his skeleton out of alignment. He glanced into the front parlour at the small tables with chairs and was about to suggest moving when Russell jumped off his stool and stood behind Dexter to massage his neck and shoulders. The boy's hands were strong and effective: the thumbs pressed deeply along the sides of his spinal column, up and down, up and down. Then the boy used both hands to squeeze and rub Dexter's trapezius muscles. It was quite amazing: the boy seemed to know exactly where to find the spots of tension and pressure; he used his fingers to locate the knots of inflammation and then rubbed and pushed and pressed and dug in so deeply that it became a numinous mixture of pleasure and pain—and Dexter simply submitted, closing his eyes, leaning ever forward until his head was mere inches from the surface of the bar. When he realized that he was making small groaning noises, he sat up straight and opened his eyes and that was when he saw that all eyes in the bar were trained on him: the two lone men, the red-faced man and boy, and Ed. Ed's gaze in particular could only be described as one of curious suspicion.

"Thank you, Russell. Thank you. That was therapeutic to say the least."

"I could do better. That shirt material is real heavy. When we go home I'll give you a good rubdown. Unless you want to give me one."

Dexter was about to respond that it wouldn't be necessary, about to reiterate that his neck and shoulders felt far better, when he saw Jean Paul standing in the hallway at the doorway. Dexter barely had time to reach for a cigarette before Jean Paul strutted into the room like a vamp in a 1940's celluloid melodrama.

"Look who's here for high tea," he said. "Ed, my usual. *Per favore.*" Jean Paul wore a navy blazer, grey flannel slacks, a pink, button-down, oxford-cloth shirt, and a patterned club tie with the repeating design of a fraternity crest: Beta Theta Pi. Jean Paul tugged at the cuffs of his starched shirt, undid the buttons of his coat, and without acknowledging Russell's presence, perched on the stool at Dexter's left. "You said you didn't like this tired establishment, Desmonda."

Dexter consulted his watch. "I thought you had a two o'clock interview. Don't you have any ties of your own?"

"Don't change the subject. You said you had errands."

"And what does that have to do with you?"

"I can't drag you out of the house on a Saturday night for one lousy drink and I find you here on a weekday, filled to the gills, with that little whore. I can save you some time and money; he's not a very good whore because he really doesn't do anything. Do you, Russell?"

The shatter of glass startled Dexter, and before he could turn around Russell had shoved past him to lunge at Jean Paul. The boy took the lapels of Jean Paul's blazer in his hands, lifted him off the bar stool, dragged him in an arc across the floor, slammed him against the wall, loosening one of the framed hunt scenes and causing it to crash to the floor with the suddenly familiar sound of shattering glass. Ed was on his way over the top of the bar as Russell pinned Jean Paul against the wall with the palm of his left hand, and when the boy clenched his right hand into a fist and cocked it over his shoulder, Dexter jumped forward.

"Whoa, boy. Steady. Please, for me, don't." He put his hand on Russell's cocked arm, exerted the slightest pressure, coaxed him to relax.

And to his amazement, Russell listened. He had been so certain that there was nothing he could do, but Russell listened. Slowly the boy lowered his arm—he still pinned Jean Paul against the wall—but he actually lowered his cocked arm. He was pawing the ground maybe, but he was no longer rearing in the air. Dexter draped his arm over the boy's shoulder, held him from the back, caressed his chest, tugged him backwards, nuzzled his ear. At first the boy felt solid and immovable, but Dexter kept coaxing. "That's my boy; easy does it; it's all right." It was a brilliant display of dressage as he nudged the boy to the back door, through the kitchen, out onto the back steps, into the vanishing sunshine for some air. At one point Ed had started to grab one of the boy's arms but Dexter must have looked at him quite crossly because the look he got back was one of respectful intimidation.

Dexter put him in the car, then went around and got in behind the wheel. Russell sat, rigid and angry, and stared straight through the windshield until they pulled into the garage. Not one word from him the entire trip back to Dexter's house, then when the engine was shut off, when he opened the boy's door: "I should have punched the mother-fucker's lights out."

Once in the kitchen, Russell went to the larder. He disappeared inside and reappeared with the new bottle of bourbon. "You want I should make you one?" he said.

In the living room Dexter sat back on the sofa and re-moved his shoes. The alcohol had given him a false sense of energy; underneath, he knew, the jet lag lingered. Then the chimes on the mantle clock struck four, reminding him that he had planned to be in the office by seven-thirty the next morning. Russell sat at the opposite end of the sofa and kicked off his tennis shoes. He lay with his head on the arm rest and stretched out with his legs across Dexter's lap. Smiling, he reached in the front pocket of his Levis.

"I copped a joint," said the boy. He opened the pack of cigarettes, withdrew a fat, hand-rolled one, tapered at both ends.

"Where did you get that? I have to work in the morn-ing," said Dexter.

"It's reefer, man. Not acid." Russell lit the marijuana, inhaled, and handed it to Dexter. "Take a couple hits. It's creeper grass," said Russell. He spoke through clenched teeth and, though he still managed to smile, not one wisp of smoke escaped from his mouth.

The drug affected Dexter almost immediately; the feeling was pleasant and numbing, though he did have dif-ficulty focusing. Twice Russell sat forward, his legs still stretched across Dexter's lap, to administer something that he referred to as *shot guns*: he put the lit end of the cigarette in his own mouth and blew smoke in a straight, direct line into Dexter's open mouth; when he did this he put his arm on Dexter's shoulder to steady himself and moved in close. The boy's nose was less than an inch from Dexter's, so he gave him a sudden kiss, on puckered lips, and laughed.

"You feel it, don't you?" said Russell. And he laughed too.

Dexter's eyelids were heavy and he rested his head on the back of the sofa. With his eyes closed he began to rub Russell's thick, flexing legs, and when the boy did not object he gradually moved his hands up toward the crotch. Each time Russell passed the cigarette to him Dexter took a puff until it was too small to hold, when he instructed Russell to put it in the ashtray on the coffee table.

"Let's go upstairs," said Russell, "to your bedroom."

In the bedroom, Russell wanted to take a shower.

"Why don't you wait until after?" said Dexter.

"After what?" said Russell, as he stepped out of his Levis. He grinned, an impish enticement with dimples at the corners of his mouth, and ran to the bed; after peeling back the comforter and top sheet, he scampered in under the covers in his under shorts and pulled the sheet up to his neck. Dexter stripped down to his boxers, put his glasses on the night stand, and climbed into bed.

It was dusk, the room faintly lit, but Russell lay with the back of his hand across his eyes. Dexter kissed the boy's mouth, but the lips remained tightly sealed, so he stretched out beside him and explored his body under the covers. Russell's skin was soft and taut and firm. Dexter pulled down the boy's shorts and turned down the blanket. Russell's arms were thick and shapely: his biceps as round as baseballs; his nipples and chest moved steadily up and down in rhythm with his rapid breathing; his stomach was a miracle of contoured ripples; his smooth legs prickled at Dexter's touch. There might as well have been a Hallelujah chorus in the corner, a flock of white doves overhead, perfumed, red rose petals falling from the ceiling, palm fronds rustling overhead, ocean waves crashing at the foot of the bed, fireworks exploding outside the windows. Dexter pressed his index finger into the boy's navel then took the asthenic penis in his hand.

***

For two weeks Dexter hurried home from work precisely at five o'clock; he searched the crowded platform at the Fullerton exit for that face; he descended the steps, hoping to see it at the turnstile exit; he walked to the corner, crossed the DePaul campus, searched around every corner and behind every tree for that smile. Each evening he hurried across his street, looked up at his front steps, hoped against hope that the boy might be waiting at the front door. He stood on his porch, still glancing over his shoulder for a sign of him; he entered his living room, dropped his briefcase, ran to his phone to check his answering machine. Then he went to the kitchen, looked through the back window, expecting to see him in the alley at the back fence. But, alas, there was no sign of Russell. None whatsoever. The boy had vanished like a dandelion gone to seed, its feathery puffs carried aloft and out of sight by a wind too cold for spring.

Dexter had great difficulty concentrating at the office, slept poorly at night, and had even gone for two consecutive Friday and Saturday evenings to The Earl. There was a different bartender so he was unable to ask about Russell, but even if Ed had been there so too was Jean Paul, and Dexter didn't wish for his friend to see his pain.

Now, hearing the front door being opened, he wished for a miracle. Jean Paul smiled, handed him the stack of envelopes and supermarket fliers. "You used to be such a fanatic about the mail," said Jean Paul. "You must have stepped right over it."

Dexter loosened his tie and sat in the wing back chair and looked down at his lap. "I had hoped for some real spring weather before I left for Trinidad."

Jean Paul laughed. "That's amusing—considering the climate in the Caribbean." Dexter smiled but said nothing. "I have a third interview at the Baron tomorrow," said Jean Paul. "You may be rid of me soon. Cocktail?"

Dexter nodded as Debit leapt onto his lap and settled on top of the stack of mail. "Put the Sibelius on while you're up," said Dexter. "The Second Symphony. That's the one you like, isn't it?" Credit vaulted onto his lap too, and Dexter stroked the two cats, using both hands. The outside temperature had fallen so steadily that he had been forced to turn the furnace back on; the air in the house was now quite dry and small snaps of static electricity jumped from the animals' fur. When Jean Paul handed him the drink, Dexter looked up and said: "Cats are a very good judge of character. Did you know?"

"Desmonda, you simply can't allow yourself to become attached to these types. That much I do know."

Dexter pushed his pets off onto the floor. He sorted through the mail then, except for the letter from American Express, put them to one side. "Stay as long as you like," said Dexter. "There's sufficient room."

Jean Paul smiled, crinkling the skin around his eyes, and looked down at his glass, angling his head in a way that allowed Dexter to see through his thinning hair to the scalp. A few days ago Jean Paul had changed his color—the reddish tint was more appropriate for a chestnut horse than for someone with his pale complexion—but Dexter had pretended not to notice. Jean Paul swirled the ice in his drink, then put the rim to his mouth. Dexter stared at the face he had known now for more than twenty years. What was it about aging that made a person's lips disappear? The ears, Dexter had heard, and the nose for that matter, continued to grow for as long as a person lived. But what was with the lips? Was there a biological reason for lips, full and plump and florid, to recede and wither and fade until there was nothing left but a horizontal slit?

It wasn't until the Friday following Russell's last visit that Dexter noticed that the credit card was missing. He was usually quite well organized; at first he thought he must have simply misplaced it, but then the call came from Marshall Field's: "Your son is here; he says you have authorized this purchase of stereo equipment."

And he had decided to approve the transaction; he had started to say: *Put my boy on the phone.* But the clerk came back on the line and said he was gone, and when Dexter called the credit card office he discovered that Russell had already charged two round trip tickets to Hawaii, four nights of hotel in Honolulu, two trips to Memphis, and more than $500 worth of clothes.

Large drops of rain splashed against the front, bay window. The streetlight in front of the house was out again. Sometimes, in the arc of its illumination, Dexter found it difficult to distinguish between rain and snow. There was a point, a brief moment as the temperature fell, when condensation glinted icy and silver during its transformation from clear to white. The light confused him. For all Dexter knew, away from the glass and the warmth of the house, it might be snowing right now. But he couldn't be sure: it was dark, and the streetlight was out.

Machu Picchu

It had only taken a few seconds for the world he had abandoned to open its doors and receive him again without question... He had regained his future.
—Mario Vargas Llosa, *The Time of the Hero.*

Dexter didn't wake up until they were directly over the Andes. There was no reason to look outside: from the moment their DC-8 lifted off the runway in Chicago there had been a dense cloud cover, and once the plane reached its cruising altitude of 35,000 feet it was night already and the cabin lights were on. After half an hour or so of uneasy conversation with Antonio, Dexter had gone searching for a row of unoccupied seats so that he could stretch out. He read the book on Peru—managed to finish all 265 pages of it despite his preoccupation with other matters—before stuffing the flat, foam pillow into the wedge between the seat and the armrest. Up the aisle Antonio was talking to the muscular steward with the pitted complexion. Dexter lay on his side, head below the window, legs bent at the knee, pulled the blanket up to his neck, and fell asleep. It was the morning beverage service cart, moving at battering ram speed and piloted by the same beefy steward, that snagged his shoeless foot and woke him.

He sat up, rubbed his toes, and accepted the glass of orange juice. The boy had removed his uniform jacket and rolled up the sleeves of his white shirt, showing his tattoo— four blue-stemmed red roses entwined around a sword—in the middle of his left forearm. Didn't the airlines frown on such things? Dexter took a sip of juice and looked out the window. Gray, jagged peaks, lit by the rising sun, poked aggressively through the clouds. The plane barely cleared the crest of muted, icy mountains. He pressed his forehead against the cold square of plastic and closed his eyes and didn't move until he felt the hand on his shoulder.

"He was nothing," said Antonio. "You know I love you." Dexter sat back from the window, turned, and looked into the widely-set, blue eyes. "We're going to have a great trip," continued Antonio. "Professor Davis said they only found women's bones at Machu Picchu."

"Maybe it was a shopping mall," said Dexter, turning away.

***

In Lima, the airport terminal was lined by uniformed soldiers—armed with machine guns and spaced mere yards apart. Thin Indian boys, fifteen or sixteen-years-old, dark-skinned with high cheekbones and slits for eyes. Mere youths. Their guns were too large not to be mounted on military trucks and the boys too young to have developed any judgment as to how or when to use such weapons. Dexter met one's glance, and the boy averted his eyes.

"So much for their men in uniform," said Antonio.

Dexter moved his head in a circular motion, but his neck was too tight from the night of cramped sleep to crack. After a few moments of silent navigation toward customs and the baggage claim area, Dexter glanced at his friend. His lids were puffy and sleep had accumulated in the corners of his eyes, but his facial muscles were relaxed.

Calm, untroubled, serene. Without remorse? A month earlier, technically four weeks ago, Antonio admitted that Kevin was gay and not simply a friend from the ski club and he made this confession only after Dexter discovered the negatives from their trip to Devil's Head and had the more suspicious ones printed. The telling picture was one of the two standing in full ski gear, each with a can of beer in his grip, posturing in front of Dexter's BMW against a background of drifting snow, their arms draped over each other's shoulder in a pose of brotherly, if not incestuous love. Well.

A pentagram on the World Atlas map; Dexter expected Lima to resemble Los Angeles. It was, after all, a city near the coast, nestled at the base of a great range of mountains and like Los Angeles it faced the Pacific Ocean and had been settled by the Spanish. And both were plagued by earthquakes. But that's where the comparison stopped. The taxi ride proceeded from the airport in late afternoon through a crowded and smoky industrial zone, then skirted the hillside barriadas and entered a tarnished city that revealed little of its colonial splendor. The avenues were broad, but not lined with palms, and choked with dilapidated cars instead of expensive European imports. The interior of the Hotel Bolivar, on the Plaza San Martín, was as close as it came to elegance, but noise from the streets found its way inside. In the public areas an attempt to mask the hotel's aging, with white paint trimmed in gold, had been made and there were crystal chandeliers and flower arrangements in the ornate, domed lobby, but the room itself was worn and dreary.

The bed creaked when Dexter lay down and sagged unhappily as Antonio crawled in next to him. Dexter turned onto his side with his back to his friend and studied the room. The top layer of beige paint peeled on the crown molding, revealing the previous choice, dull green, and a sepia water stain, shaped like a Rorschach alpaca, started on the ceiling close to the window and continued down the wall. The window in this room had been replaced with a thick, immovable pane, gapped a few inches at the bottom to let in outside air, the temperature of which stayed relatively constant in the coastal areas. Pollution or noise had not been a consideration in the refitting.

"No cuddling?" said Antonio. Dexter felt the arm encircle his chest and the weight of Antonio's thick thigh as it came to rest on his hip.

"Let's take a nap," said Dexter, "then go down for some dinner." He gave token resistance before allowing Antonio to turn him over on his back, and when his friend kissed his ear, worked his way slowly, full of breath, down the side of his neck and onto his chest, Dexter closed his eyes and tried to picture brighter times. What he got was an image of Phil. The penultimate affair. Muddy green eyes and overdeveloped trapezius muscles; he and Antonio worked out together in the YMCA weight room. Dexter came home from work early and found them standing naked in front of the bedroom mirror, grinning foolishly, their hands clasped around each other's biceps.

***

The sidewalks were empty. No affluent citizens promenading in this city. Dexter stood across the street from the Bolivar's side entrance. Amber light from inside the second floor cocktail lounge contrasted with the darkness of the street. He looked up, found their room, and saw Antonio's silhouette as he crossed in front of the drapery sheers in his undershorts. When the room went dark, Dexter started west toward the plaza.

Neon lights—reds, yellows, blues, and greens—blinked and flashed from rooftop scaffolds around the circle, and the statue of Peru's liberator, Jose de San Martín, watched on horseback from the center as autos sped around him. Dexter zipped his jacket to the neck. It was June, the beginning of winter and the night air was thick with dampness. He'd done research for the trip—he knew the locals called this phenomenon the *garúa*—but this excursion had been Antonio's idea and he simply hadn't the enthusiasm to read and plan as he did before most of his travels to exotic places. He came home from the office, found Antonio in the kitchen at the table, brochures and airplane schedules fanned out before him. "We need to spend more time together," he said, as if Dexter were the one who had immersed himself in extracurricular affairs, "and you said you wanted to see Machu Picchu." He stood, came over to Dexter, and put the full-color picture of the mountaintop ruins on the counter. "You look so handsome in your new suit," he said, and kissed him on the cheek. Then he stripped off his tank top and stepped out of his gym shorts and leaned into him, his smooth pecs pressed against Dexter's lapels.

After a few blocks, he became aware of his companion—smiling and friendly. Whenever and wherever Dexter glanced, he saw him: in the doorway, a few steps behind, parallel on the other side of the street. He was there in the park too and on the path high above the Pacific in Miraflores, and finally, once the young mestizo stood adjacent, leaning against the pipe railing next to him, Dexter spoke.

"*Buenas noches.*"

"American?" The boy smiled. The fluorescent street light flickered and a full moon lit the ocean. Dexter smiled back and the boy moved closer. Waves crashed hard against the rocks below. The boy was young but his teeth were brown. "*Coca, Señor? Cocaína?*"

***

After a leisurely walk under cloud cover to the National Library, and cursory visits to the three museums that featured Indian and Spanish colonial art, pre-Columbian archaeology, and colonial history—all of which consumed the lesser part of two days—Antonio became bored. On the third day, he didn't simply linger over his morning coffee, he dawdled, blowing on the black liquid even after it was as cold as ink, before reluctantly following Dexter to the Plaza de Armas, the old central square laid out by Lima's founder, Francisco Pizarro. Lacking even the pretense of a dilettante, he slogged through the cathedral as though his feet were encased in mud-laden boots, and later when Dexter stopped at the edge of the park to stare up at the Municipal Building, Antonio stood, listless, a child locked in a room without toys.

Dexter consulted the pamphlet, then pointed to the Presidential residence. "That's where Pizarro's palace once stood," he said.

"Don't you want to try any of the bars?" said Antonio. Dexter turned away from him and into the sun. He walked until he reached the Archbishop's palace, glanced once more at his tourist brochure, then took note of the splendidly carved wooden balconies of Moorish design. Antonio stepped in front of Dexter, picked a fallen leaf off of his jacket, grinned, and said: "If we see him tonight, can I get some?"

***

Three hundred and fifty miles east of Lima, in an Andean valley at an elevation of 11,440 feet, lay Cuzco, the ancient capital of the Incan empire. Dexter sat on the bench in the central square, another Plaza de Armas, and admired the church built by the Spanish colonists. The sun bathed its two domed towers in golden light, and he reached into the inner pocket of his jacket for sunglasses. The ten minute walk from their small hotel, up the narrow street and past the wall of massive and mortarless, hewn stones, had not only winded him but also left him with a slight headache—concentrated in the sinus cavity, just above the eyebrows. Antonio had refused to come with him, saying that the early morning breakfast made him too queasy to eat, the 8:00 A.M. flight left him too tired to go sightseeing.

Last night in bed, after it became clear that Dexter would never buy cocaine at ten dollars, or eight dollars, or even four dollars a gram, Antonio pushed away, rolled over and clung to his side of the bed like an angry wife who has banished her husband to the den. Dexter explained that these boys were usually working for the police in an effort to entrap naïve visitors, especially Americans, and had he purchased even the minutest quantity, there would probably have been a late-night knock on their hotel room door. Antonio sniffed. Then, when Dexter reminded him of the trouble cocaine had caused him and his pledge to not do it ever again, Antonio answered in a whining shrill that he didn't see why since they were on vacation that they couldn't make an exception. Finally, when Antonio was unable to massage Dexter into submission, he had shoved him with his fist, knuckles against vertebrae, rolled over, and said: "I wish we'd gone to Rio."

Dexter made his way back to the hotel, altering his route in order to see more of the town. Many of the homes had been constructed in the Spanish style upon the Inca foundations. Most of these foundations, like the walls throughout the city, had been constructed five hundred years earlier by the Incas when Cuzco was at the height of its development. The stones, often several feet in length and height and weighing tons, were irregular in shape and fitted together so perfectly that they had withstood severe earthquakes without damage while more recent Spanish structures had been seriously damaged or even destroyed.

He stopped at the desk to get the room key, then climbed the stairs to the second story. Inside, the bed was mussed and both suitcases lay open on the floor, but the room was empty. He stepped over the threshold, closed the door, and walked into the bathroom: dampness floated in the air like a vapor. The mirror was fogged; both of the thin, white bath towels had been used, then crammed carelessly back on the towel rack, and the khaki-colored chinos and pale blue button-down shirt that Antonio had worn on the flight were discarded in a pile on the floor next to the shower. Dexter stood for a moment staring at the vanity now cluttered with articles from Antonio's shaving kit—nail clippers, dental floss, toothpaste, deodorant, cologne, moisturizer for his skin, and lip balm—then he straightened the towels, picked up the trousers and shirt, and went back into the bedroom. He checked the top of the dresser and the desk for a note, but found none. Still holding Antonio's clothes, he sat on the edge of the bed in a patch of sun and looked out the window onto the stone-paved, narrow street. Four Indian boys, talking and laughing among themselves, crossed under him—their straight, black hair glistening in the light. The smallest of them shoved one of his friends at the shoulder and called him a name and took off running, and when the others broke into laughter, Dexter watched as they too raced up the sidewalk and around the corner of the stone wall.

There was a small, black jar on the nightstand—something called *Glossaire* that Antonio used in his hair to make it shine. Dexter picked it up and removed the lid, then put the fist-sized container of gel under his nose and inhaled. The aroma of orange blossoms drifted into his nostrils.

***

At the restaurant, Dexter chose a table by the window and ordered a bottle of the locally-brewed Cusqueña and waited for his meal. His pamphlet disclosed the facts about the special train line that had been built to make Machu Picchu accessible, but he only read for a minute or so at a time before looking up and out the window. He'd left a note himself, with a sketch of town that indicated the restaurant's location, in case Antonio returned. But Dexter finished reading the brochure—there was one train a day, the trip was fifty miles northwest from Cuzco, it took just over three hours and cost fifty dollars—and there was no sign of Antonio. He finished his Ají de Gallina and boiled yuccas, wiping a dribble of red chili sauce off his chin, and ordered another Cusqueña and finished that too—and still no Antonio.

He stood, lightheaded, in the doorway of the restaurant and checked his map for the best route to the train station. Advance reservations were necessary. The group of boys he had seen from the room were walking toward him on the walk; there were five of them now and the new boy was considerably taller and larger than the others. Dexter smiled as they passed, but except for the new member who frowned, they seemed not to notice. He stepped into the street, turned left, and headed uphill. The combination of altitude, alcohol, and a full stomach was formidable, and Dexter walked slowly, lifting first his left and then his right foot as methodically as a llama overloaded with woven blankets for the marketplace, and by the time he reached the level cross street at the top of the incline, his head was throbbing like a hide-covered drum.

He paused to catch his breath, checked the map again, and looked down the street. He'd expected to see the Indian boys, receding in the distance, not Antonio. A patch of dark, reddish purple: Antonio had packed a plum-colored polo; the figure was at the end of the second block, just below the horizon, and then it vanished from view. Was it really him? Dexter picked up his pace for a minute or two, until his throat burned and his lungs ached for oxygen, but he didn't stop. He pushed onward, arriving at the spot, as nearly as he could judge, where the person had been. He could see for four, maybe five blocks ahead; the cobble-stone street continued its downward slope before curving to the left. No Antonio. Dexter proceeded to the next inter-section and located it on the map. Going right would take him downhill and toward the edge of town, while the street to the left, which appeared busier with shoppers and tour-ists, led up to Sacsayhuaman, the extensive Inca fortress established on the hill above Cuzco. He had only begun to make his ascent up the street, toward the pre-Columbian site, when Antonio emerged from a doorway in the middle of the next block.

Dexter watched. Antonio stood on the sidewalk, glanced to his right in the direction of Sacsayhuaman, then turned around to face the building he had come out of. There was no doubt about it even at this distance. Anto-nio's curly hair, the purple shirt and faded Levis, the wide shoulders, thick neck, and his muscular arms, held out and away from the sides of his body as if he were poised to pull one of the unwieldy stones from its place in the founda-tion—all of this contrasted dramatically with the appearance of other tourists and the local inhabitants. Dexter thrust his right arm in the air and opened his mouth to yell and that's when the second thickset figure stepped, no, jumped from the same doorway and threw his arms around Antonio and hugged him, jostled him, right there in the middle of the stone-paved area, oblivious to passersby. Indeed. Then when Antonio looked in both directions before slapping the brawny boy on the back, Dexter moved away from the center of the street to hide behind a rack of postcards outside a souvenir shop.

As Antonio and the other started up the street, side by side and as symmetrical as two carved Intis, Dexter moved to close the distance between them and himself. Mindful that Antonio might turn in his direction at any time, he followed but hugged the facade of storefronts and kept behind other tourists whenever possible. When Dexter came to the place where he had first seen Antonio, he saw that it was a hotel, very small, and apparently modest. Similar, in fact, to the one he had chosen. Knowing that Antonio had met someone at a hotel—in a city where before this morning he'd never been—was at once a source of confusion and inspiration. Confusing for obvious reasons: Who was he? Where had he come from? How had Antonio met him? Inspiring because after fifteen minutes of physical exertion, Dexter actually managed to get within a few yards of them without being discovered, and that was when, finally close enough to see the boy's pockmarked face and the etched roses on his forearm, that he understood who Antonio's companion was—and the circumstances that had probably brought him to Cuzco.

The revelation chilled him like a friaje sweeping unexpected from the Amazon basin into the mountains, and after another fifteen minutes, Dexter began to lag. He simply was no match for the altitude, let alone Antonio and the muscle-bound steward. Even the natives moved slowly, and Dexter was now breathing so heavily and was so tired that he was forced to stop before continuing up the hill. When he looked up, Antonio and the friend were gone.

Dexter had never followed anyone before, and it seemed wrong and disagreeable: the type of behavior that could turn obsessive if left unchecked: like stalking or skulking behind a row of lockers to peer into the showers at the YMCA. Had he been afraid of what he'd find? Dexter turned and retraced his route, away from Sacsayhuaman, away from Antonio.

After awhile he discovered Calle Loreto. Long and broad by Cuzco standards, it was a wide, level and unimpeded thoroughfare that enabled pedestrians to get from one place to another efficiently, but there were no shops here and as a result, few people. The surface of Calle Loreto was cobbled and rough—in contrast to the smooth, perfectly fitted and tapered walls that enclosed it. Walls twenty feet high, and like the others in the city, a foundation for more recent Spanish architecture. Dexter started down the street. Twenty or thirty yards along, on the left, he came to a massive, arched portal in the wall fitted with a heavy, wooden door, large enough to accommodate a truck. But this door it seemed was seldom opened for another smaller opening, a door within a door just large enough for one person to step in or out of the interior space, was used. An Indian sat on the step holding a handcrafted, stringed instrument. The size of a double bass with a triangular-shaped soundboard, it had four circular holes and a long, narrow fingerboard. The musician leaned against the blue surface of the door, a plastic cup of coins next to his sandal-clad feet. His neck stretched back and his head canted at an angle—as if he were looking to some ancient god of the sun for inspiration before he plucked a single string. Then Dexter saw: the man was blind—the whites of his eyes were yellow, the irises milky. Dexter reached into his pocket and pulled out a fistful of coins and dropped them in the cup. The musician didn't react. Was he asleep or in a trance?

There was only Dexter and the idle musician. No one else. Far ahead, where the walls narrowed to a pinpoint opening, a trick of perspective, several figures appeared, coming into view as if at the end of a long tunnel. There were many colors in the walls, but muted. Here, in the shaded part, the rock was cool—blue and flecked with silver—and there were only faint traces of warmer, rosier hues, but in the distance where the sun lit the street and angled across the northern wall it was as if the rocks had been quarried from a different mountain. The colors were still somber, but redder and more yellow. Golden. Dexter tilted back his head too and gazed up at the clear sky. A narrow strip of white light. He walked on, looking up into the pale atmosphere. Dexter was alone. Alone in the street, alone in the city, alone with his thoughts. Alone.

And then there were others. He realized later: four or five others; he'd seen them before. Shoving at him, pressing him against the wall. Their putrid odor permeated the air, and Dexter had to choose between not breathing or gagging. The smell of poverty. One was on his knees and grabbing at Dexter's cuffs, feeling his ankles. Another's hands reached in his hip pockets while others probed at his shirt. He couldn't move; the largest boy pinned him against the wall, his fingers and thumb clutched at Dexter's throat. He covered the right, front pocket of his trousers with one hand—that's where his wallet was—and shoved at the largest boy with his other. Dexter yelled: "No. No. No." And the thief smiled and said something in a language, a dialect, that Dexter did not understand. And then the other boys began to yell.

Dexter screamed as loudly as he could: a sustained, primeval call for help. The boy let go of his throat and placed both his hands on Dexter's chest and patted and smiled as if to reassure him. "*Lo siento, Señor,*" he said, nodding. "*Lo siento.*" His coruscant eyes, black as chunks of obsidian, pried Dexter. Never mind that this boy's eyes were dark while Antonio's were blue, or that these lashes were straight and not curled, or that these eyes slanted down at the edges while Antonio's slanted up. Never mind. They were as similar as a jaguar from the Amazon and a California cougar, this boy and Antonio. A different species perhaps, but they were the same animal, the same creature. The same.

All of them had stepped back now, following their leader's example. All of them were smiling too and nodding. And bowing. As if they could somehow, someway, convince Dexter that this had been a mistake. They had simply run into him. Bumped him, as if in the middle of a crowded market, they seemed to be saying. And when Dexter yelled again, yelled until his throat was raw, yelled until all the blood in his body was centered in his larynx, yelled until he started to choke and then slid down the surface of the wall with his head in his hands, yelled until he began to cry, they ran.

***

Inti Raymi was the Inca winter solstice celebration, and conveniently for the Spanish it coincided with the Catholic feast of St. John the Baptist and the events had been transferred to an ostensibly Christian fiesta. Dexter found the hotel room exactly as he had left it. He undressed and fell into bed as the sun disappeared and he slept through this longest night of the year without waking. Fires burned throughout the night—fires to bring back the sun— and the following day Sacsayhuaman was crowded with campesinos, townspeople, and travelers who gathered in the sunshine to watch the music and dance groups perform.

Dexter would have been surprised to find him in bed beside him when he awoke, would have been surprised to see him come through the door at breakfast, in fact. And even though he'd taken the route past the steward's hotel on his way to the train station, he hadn't really considered trying to find Antonio. Any business they had could wait.

The floor of the open fortress was enormous, hardened and smooth from the hundreds of dancers and musicians who had come to celebrate, and the thousands of observers who had walked across the center to sit on bleachers or to climb onto the stones that terraced the hillsides. After making the single reservation for Machu Picchu, Dexter had come here and now sat on a rock near the ground.

When a group of six musicians began to play directly in front of him, an equal number of dancers, three men and three women, wearing layers of clothing in every possible color, joined in. The musicians were all men—two of them played guitars, and a third played a much smaller stringed instrument; it was smaller even than a violin and played without a bow: he plucked and strummed it in an intricate rhythm of rapid and almost inconceivable velocity. Percussion was provided by a simple, deep-voiced frame drum played with a hide-padded stick; the small boy thumped the drumhead, his expression unfailingly studious and peaceful. There was a flute too, notched and carved of wood, and the sound that came from it was haunting and melancholy, but the panpipes, oh the panpipes... There were seven pipes bound together, varied in length—the longest perhaps a foot, the smallest no more than three inches—and the boy blew across the end of the pipes with astonishing dexterity producing a breathy sound, as high-pitched as a bird call, then as deep as the voice of a bassoon. He played a kind of complex duet, alternating single notes of a smooth-flowing melody, never missing a beat. It was magical and intoxicating, utterly characteristic of the Andes, evoking the cool breeze that swirled down from the surrounding blue and sunlit peaks.

Dexter scooted forward, then dropped down to sit on a lower stone, closer to the musicians and dancers. The dancers were whirling, stamping their feet, and yelling—the women's patterned, ruffled skirts of pink and black and yellow and blue and green stood out as they gathered speed—their arms held out away from their sides, the rhythm was infectious and insistent. The dancers, like the musicians, did not smile, but their joy was apparent; it was as if they had been born to dance, as if their entire history were summed up in this frenzied and glorious ritual.

Then one of the girls looked at Dexter, and, without breaking stride, smiled—a warm and friendly smile, as inviting as a mother's embrace. She dropped her partner's hand and reached out to Dexter, and he reached back and allowed her to pull him off the rock and into their circle. And he began to dance. Cautiously at first, stepping slowly up and down, then faster and faster until he matched the rhythm, their rhythm. Spinning and whirling and stomping, he danced. And he laughed. "*Más fuerza!*" the girl yelled. "*Más fuerza!*" And Dexter danced harder, and the music pounded and pulsed and plunged and soared, lifting him high over the puna, high over the icy, snow-covered Andes, high above the earth, higher than he'd ever been before.

Tula

Dexter entered his office, put the mug of fresh coffee on his drink coaster.

And noticed the phone messages.

Amazed, as he'd only been gone a minute or two at most, he picked up the yellow slips of paper from the front edge of the desk blotter pad; there were five separate message forms: one of the calls was personal, two were from co-workers—and two were from the new Chief Auditor who had called Dexter twice. Dexter hurried around his desk and dropped into his chair, prepared to take immediate action. Everyone in the office knew: in a crisis, you could count on Dexter Giles: when he saw storm clouds on the horizon, he opened an umbrella.

And then he noticed yesterday's date on the first slip.

He flipped it to the back and checked the second message. Yesterday's date. He checked the third. Yesterday. And the fourth. Yesterday. He didn't bother to look at the fifth. He picked up a pad of paper, rushed out of the office, turned left, and strode down the floor past the office cubicles next to the lakeside windows. At the northeast corner of the floor, outside the Chief Auditor's office, sat Tula, deliverer of messages. As much as the woman tried to affect elegance, with her cocktail rings and jingling bracelets and blackened false eyelashes, she looked like a waitress in a Greek restaurant on the corner of Jackson and Halsted, and he could picture her in a gaudy skirt, a tray of flaming saginaki perched on fingertips, making her way among oil-cloth-covered tables.

"Is there a reason that I'm just now getting these messages?" said Dexter, standing in front of her, pad in one hand, the yellow slips crumpled in the other.

"You got a copy of Mr. Gastineau's memo," said Tula, arching symmetrical eyebrows which had been plucked to baldness then methodically pencilled back in. She stiffened in her chair and said: "'Until installation of the new voice mail system has been completed, auditors are to periodically check in at the secretary's station for phone messages.'"

"'To facilitate the delivery of them, which will be twice daily.' These are from yesterday. Mr. Gastineau rang me twice. Is he busy?"

She glared at Dexter, then swiveled away to shuffle the papers on her desk—turning two letters face down in a move contrived for effect rather than out of any legitimate need for confidentiality—and when at last she reached lazily for the telephone Dexter walked with insouciance to the windows on the north side to demonstrate that he had no interest in her mundane, secretarial duties.

The only enclosed offices at the floor's perimeter were at the four corners; the side areas of the Imperial Building were open, separated by acoustically carpeted panels, and reserved for younger, lower-ranking staff members. The boy who normally occupied the space where Dexter stood, a green-eyed graduate whose lean physique had yet to be ruined by years of meat and potato and beer lunches, was on an audit assignment in Houston. Dexter looked down at the sprawl of architecture, studying the grid of water storage tanks and air conditioning systems on the roofs of the older and smaller towers. Vapors swirled in the seething August air.

He walked back to the area outside the Chief Auditor's office, and Tula spoke without looking up from her typewriter. "He'll see you now."

"Thank you." Dexter made an abrupt, sarcastic bow, then stepped inside the man's office and smiled.

"Sorry I took so long to get back to you, Ernie."

"Sit down, Dexter. Coffee?"

Dexter shook his head.

"I'm afraid I'm going to have to ask you to postpone the Argentina audit—and your vacation. Something has come up." Gastineau leaned back in his leather chair and drummed his fingers on the armrest. His eyebrows were the antithesis to those of his secretary; so coarse, thick, and long were they that one was easily distracted from the achromatic gray of his irises. Looks aside, Dexter found the chubby man likeable despite his lack of experience in internal auditing and despite the fact that he was rather self-indulgent. The latter characteristic was probably unavoidable: in a company as large as Imperial Petroleum anyone who advanced quickly went through a period of ego inflation. This man was no exception; he had grown up in an Iowa town with fewer people than this company had lawyers.

"No problem, sir. What's the scoop?" said Dexter. He placed the pad on his lap, withdrew his gold Cross pen from its pocket protector, and immediately wrote his initials in the upper right hand corner of the page. Then the heading: *Conversation with E. Gastineau on 8-15.*

Here, the man leaned back in his chair and stretched to retrieve a file folder from the credenza against the wall. "T and E Review of Marketing," said Gastineau, eyebrows dancing to emphasize key syllables. "The outside auditors have agreed to let us do it in-house." Dexter nodded knowingly. "It'll save on the audit fee and—"

"Keep them out of our business," said Dexter, nodding more vigorously.

"Exactly," said Gastineau. He began to outline the scope and schedule of the project; the review was to focus on the vice president, members of the marketing committee, and the regional managers; Dexter was to perform the audit alone, he was to discuss his progress with no one, and not a single person should by privy to any findings—except for Gastineau, who would of course be required to work closely with Dexter on a supervisory basis; timely completion of the review would be crucial. "Start immediately," said Gastineau. "Any questions?"

Dexter stood to leave and had taken three steps toward the door when his boss spoke again. "Oh, and don't go to word processing with this. Have Tula type the memoranda."

Dexter turned to face him. "Tula, sir? Might I suggest Doris. She has thirty years of service and she's quite discreet. It would—"

"No, I want Tula on this."

"Fine." Dexter took three more steps toward the door.

"It's not a big thing, Dexter, but—"

Dexter turned again.

"When I phone, try to get back to me sooner. It's kind of a thing with me. I believe in returning calls promptly."

Blood surged into Dexter's face and head. His bare scalp was suddenly quite tender, as if he had stayed in the sun too long, and when he stepped outside Gastineau's office, he was met by Tula's long nose and close-set eyes. She perched on the front of her desk, grinning: a carrion bird, holding a dead carcass in her talons and tearing the flesh from its bones.

***

Only a fool would spend twenty-five years as a man's mistress and think there was any future in it. It wasn't his fault that she had hitched her star to the wrong wagon. It wasn't his fault that her boss had been a thief.

And a stupid thief.

Dexter stood in the vault staring at the stack of expense reports.

And now she was bitter and impossible.

He carried the reports—a sample drawn from the last three years—to the desk just outside the vault. Each form was stuffed with receipts, which testified to nights of lavish entertainment; each form was punctured and secured by scores of staples—to discourage prying of course—and it took him several minutes just to get the paper unfolded. The marketing vice president, a charmless man who wandered throughout his department smearing clerks and secretaries with his patronizing smiles, reportedly had a drinking problem; stories of him attending meetings, in a drunken condition, abounded. These guys in the rarefied air could get away with so much—but only the greedy had to steal.

And she wanted retribution; she wanted to destroy him.

Dexter removed the final staple and studied the first receipt: Blackmore had hosted ten people for dinner at the Midway Club. The purpose: *Business Development in the Central Division.* The tab: $2,000.

He may have contributed to her lover's demise and his audit may have provided the impetus for the man's early retirement, but he would not accept the responsibility for her transfer to auditing. Perhaps he should march into Gastineau's office and spell it out: "Ernie, my audit ended her lover's career. She wants my hide."

Dexter took off his glasses and rubbed his eyes.

And growled aloud: "If she wants war, so be it."

***

He stepped off the bus, walked east on Diversey, re-playing time and again the day's three separate conversations with Tula. He had entered the supply room and taken a pad of lined paper down from the shelf, and as he had turned to leave, she had come into the room. He waited for her to pass, then moved to the door. He was framed in the entry, seconds from escape, when he heard her raspy voice:

"No memos on the audit yet?"

"You know you really ought to lay off the Marlboros," said Dexter. "You're starting to sound like Raymond Burr."

"You've dyed your hair, haven't you?" said Tula.

He turned to face her. "What hair I have left is natural, but thanks for the compliment."

He wheeled and stepped out of the ill-ventilated space before she could respond. But later the same day, when he deposited a memo on her desk for typing, she had said:

"You just missed a phone call from your boyfriend." She extended the slip of paper. "I was about to dash back with it when I saw you coming this way."

"Good girl. I imagine the last time you dashed was into Marshall Field's basement for that Gypsy outfit."

"Did you have your eye on it?"

In the midst of battle one does not always realize the seriousness of one's wound, and Dexter only had time to identify three possible avenues of reply: he could have said that he needed the dress for his pet monkey, or that he had been invited to a costume party, or that he had taken a job as a musician in a Turkish nightclub, but then Gastineau had come out of his office, ending the bloodshed—which was fortunate because all of Dexter's considered counter-measures were weak. He had stayed late at the office but in fact was able only to do meaningless work; his thoughts were locked inextricably on the day's two bitter, sticho-mythic exchanges with Tula. So it came as a still further surprise when he rushed around the corner at work and stepped into the elevator and found himself face to face with her yet again.

He looked her up and down and said: "Off to the mill for the night shift are we?"

In the elevator of his own building, on his way to his thirty-third floor apartment, he admitted to himself that no response would have been good enough because her re-marks amounted to an irreversible deepening of hostilities, and as he stood in the hallway and unlocked his door he understood clearly the gravity of his injury. He slipped in-side and Debit and Credit meowed loudly and began winding around and through his legs. He set down his briefcase and stooped to pet them, then went into the galley kitchen to get their food. It was only a matter of time until Tula started dropping malicious remarks in Gastineau's of-fice. Or had she already?

***

He waited behind the bank of filing cabinets which functioned as a backdrop to her work area. Tula had lined the top of the cabinets with an assortment of her own potted plants, of the common, everyday variety: Boston fern, English ivy, African violet, and philodendron. And from this spot and with this camouflage, he could monitor her activities and telephone conversations—if she spoke clearly and if there were no other people in the vicinity. He pretended to study the contents of a manila folder.

"It's a twenty minute drive from the house," she said. She paused to listen, mumbled something unintelligible, then raised her voice and said, quite emphatically: "We can afford it."

Ernie Gastineau came out from his office and approached her desk. Dexter stepped to the right so that his head and shoulders were obscured by the philodendron. "I can't talk about it now," said Tula. "I'll call you later."

Gastineau asked Tula to come into his office so that he could dictate a letter; once she was inside and the door had been closed, Dexter approached her desk and removed the contents of her in-basket.

***

Ernie Gastineau was not one of the boys. There was nothing particularly charismatic about him—he was overweight, fifty or so, and except for the eyebrows, the most noticeable feature of his smooth, white face was the weak chin. Ernie's wife and two weak-chinned children were plump as well; when Mrs. Gastineau came into the office with them Dexter had to exercise considerable restraint not to stare as they looked a great deal more like sisters and brothers as they waddled in: the same shape, the same coloring, the same manner of speech. It was easy to picture the family neatly arranged in their Peugeot leaving their upscale tract house and on the way to church, leaning in unison into the curves taken gingerly by their oh-so-careful and cautious patriarch. Ernie played golf, but that was the only thing he had in common with middle management of Imperial, and Dexter realized what Ernie Gastineau did not: internal auditing was for losers. Losers. Computer geeks, bachelors, the poorly-groomed, the unattractive, the unathletic, the out-of-shape, the minorities, and the straight-laced if you will.

Ernie leaned forward to accept the printouts from Dexter. "You'll probably have to get used to the size of the numbers," said Dexter. "I reviewed for proper documentation: the guests, their titles and positions, the nature of the business discussion; I've summarized total travel and entertainment by month for the last three years on the last six sheets. In terms of IRS regs, there are some definite problems."

"Thirty thousand dollars for one dinner?" said Ernie, his complexion suddenly pale, his expression suddenly sober, as if pornographic pictures of teenage girls had fallen out of his briefcase in full view of his wife.

Dexter shook his head. "Marketing types always seem to think it's part of their job description to spend huge sums of money." Ernie Gastineau thumbed through the sheets of paper: forward, backwards, then forward again. Dexter leaned back in his chair, crossed his legs at the knee, and regarded the filigreed design on the toe of his polished shoe. "I've often thought we should establish a standard ratio for sales people. They should generate, say, a thousand times more in sales than they spend for entertainment. Anyone who falls consistently below should be shown the door. All the way to the top too."

Ernie Gastineau looked up and parted his lips as if to speak but merely squinted.

"Reads like a Harold Robbins novel, doesn't it?" said Dexter. When, after at least a full sixty seconds, Gastineau still did not speak, he continued. "Granted, the elk hunt is questionable, seeing as how we have absolutely no marketing outlets in the West. Of course you don't see the whole story there. A contact of mine in the marketing department was instructed to arrange the trip." Dexter glanced at his nails and straightened his tie. "He says Blackmore took along someone named Denise Daley, but don't expect to find pictures."

"Denise Daley?" said Gastineau.

"A current girlfriend. She used to go out with the chairman; he passed her on when he got bored. Apparently she has a thing for oil men."

"Daley?" said Gastineau.

"No relation to *hissoner*, I'm told," said Dexter.

Gastineau sat, staring at the figures, with his mouth hanging open; even his eyebrows were sitting this one out. Dexter remained motionless in his chair too and watched as his boss finally closed his mouth and swallowed, as if flooded with saliva. When the man seemed on the verge of speaking Dexter said: "Are you familiar with the details of the Gallagher audit?"

Gastineau shook his head.

"Do you want me to close the door?"

Gastineau nodded.

Dexter walked over, looked outside, spotted Tula within earshot pulling dead leaves off a ficus tree. She glanced over, Dexter smiled, then swung the door closed with a resounding thunk.

Dexter started speaking as he walked back to his chair. "He was taking payoffs for arranging loans in the Far East. He was paid by check. We might never have caught him but he was foolish enough to deposit the checks in the bank downstairs." Gastineau looked at Dexter without expression. "We own the bank," said Dexter. "At least enough of it to give us audit privileges."

The eyebrows jerked suddenly. "Wasn't Tula—"

"Yes, she was," said Dexter. "For twenty-five years." He paused here for emphasis. "She took the checks down. Lucky for us that I saw one on her desk and started asking questions. Gallagher was given early retirement. The irony is, he was fired for his stupidity, not his malfeasance."

"No wonder she—"

"Yes," said Dexter.

Ernie Gastineau averted his gaze. "Nothing," he said.

***

On the north side of the building, over the old Illinois Central tracks, they were digging a vast hole. An array of gigantic earth-moving equipment plied the ground: some of the machinery pushed the dirt into piles, some of it climbed up onto the piles, and others dug into the same piles to deposit the earth into dump trucks—so large that the drivers were mere specks behind the windshields. Dexter stood in the window looking down. He spotted a type of equipment that he'd never seen before: a behemoth fork lift, except that instead of a loading platform or flat spears on the front it had a long shaft, and at the end of the shaft, a huge pointed spike which was directed at an angle back in and toward the operator. Like a person with a knife in their fist, the machine stabbed the ground, enabling its operator to break up the clay and bedrock. The machine was phallic to be sure and Dexter pictured Tula at the controls, using the rig to perform violent automanipulation.

And he giggled aloud.

Last night's discovery had been most satisfying. Could there be any doubt now about who would prevail? By eight o'clock everyone had gone home, leaving Dexter and the Polish cleaning woman and Tula's potted plants alone on the floor. But for the hum of the vacuum cleaner around a distant corner and the ticking of the fluorescent lights overhead there were no sounds. One could almost hear the aphids chomping the leaves of Tula's plants. Dexter had slipped his master key into the lock and pulled the drawers open, one-by-one. He searched through the stacks of papers and folders until he found the small, gray ledger at the very back and bottom of the deepest drawer. Listening to telephone conversations provided limited information. He needed evidence. And legitimate company business was always stored in the computer; find what's off-book and you know what a person is hiding. At first he had had misgivings: Tula's history was probably far more interesting that her present life. After all there was nothing illegal about being a man's mistress. Still, Ernie Gastineau was religious and Dexter was a firm believer in the practice of getting a person on whatever grounds one could. If one couldn't discredit a person on the basis of his or her performance, the smart strategy was to use politics or morality. That's what she was doing, wasn't it? Spreading rumors about his sexuality. He was the best auditing mind in the entire department and he was a good judge of character—or the lack of it. But his performance would count for little or nothing in the face of the shrew's homophobic and hysterical ranting.

It took a great deal of effort for him not to break into song, for him not to dance a celebratory jig when he realized what the ledger contained. Rent receipts, disbursements for maintenance and taxes, tenant lease forms, telephone logs. Gallagher had been banished over a year ago, but she was still running his rental property: over fifty apartments in all. He almost felt sorry for her. She did everything. The telephone calls, the copying, the mailings, the errands, the bookkeeping. And she managed the winter house on Sanibel Island too. It was the classic, textbook case of a corporate conflict-of-interest.

Dexter was still giggling as he went back into his interior, viewless office and picked up the phone.

And when it was ringing on the other end, he sat down.

And when Tula said: "Mr. Gastineau's office," Ernie's silhouette appeared outside the glass partition and then the man filled the doorway of Dexter's office.

"Beautiful day, isn't it?" said Ernie Gastineau. "So this is your home base." He glanced around and hesitated at the small bookcase before removing a book conveniently located on the shelf next to his shoulder. He examined the spine, the cover, and then the flyleaf, as if not sure whether to feign interest in the book's contents or the paper upon which it was printed. "These interior offices are really quite nice," he said as he replaced the book.

Dexter said, "Excuse the ring," hung up, and gestured toward one of the two chairs facing his desk.

"I've been reviewing the working papers on the T and E audit," he said, not making eye content.

"Yes," said Dexter.

"I'm wondering if maybe we should expand the scope of the audit—you know, go back a few more years."

"Of course that's an option," said Dexter. "But to what purpose?"

"Well, you know, to insure that we're putting things in their proper perspective. I'm sure you agree that we don't want to come off looking like we're nitpicking." Gastineau smiled, without joy, like the preacher who seems somehow too angry to be recounting the rewards of Heaven.

"You consider taking fifty people to Las Vegas for five days at a cost of $125,000 to discuss the proliferation of self service outlets to be a nit?" Dexter leaned forward, rested his elbows on the desk. "I mean what does Wayne Newton know about self service?"

Still affecting composure, Ernie Gastineau leaned on the left armrest and shifted his weight onto his left buttock. "Look Giles," he said, "Marketing had record profits last year—"

"Because of transfer pricing; the price of crude is down," said Dexter.

During the brief time that Gastineau had been at the auditing helm, Dexter had never known him to maintain eye contact for more than a second or two, but now the man tilted back his head, as if to make sure that his bushy eyebrows would not obstruct his view, and stared unblinking for several beats. The pupils themselves had grown large, the mouth tightened, the jaw clenched; even the jelly-like consistency of the man's chins seemed more rigid, more firm. The man practically sniffed the air for danger and all at once Dexter realized that he and Ernie Gastineau weren't even on the same side—they weren't even fighting a common enemy.

"The chairman approved that expenditure, was there in fact for a couple of nights: he spoke to them about the corporate, long-range plan," said Gastineau, his voice a full register lower.

"I see," said Dexter.

"And some of your working papers didn't have dates or titles on them," said Gastineau. "The outside auditors are going to want to see our documentation—and that's not the sort of thing that will make us any friends." The man reached into his jacket and extracted a memo from the inside pocket. "And there are some typos in this most recent memorandum." He put the paper down on the desk and Dexter saw that he had circled several words using a red pen. Dexter snatched the paper and examined it.

"I told Tula to make those corrections before distribution; she deliberately disobeyed my instructions—"

"Perhaps if you asked and didn't tell, your wishes wouldn't be so easily misconstrued."

***

Ernie Gastineau was activities-oriented. Not results-oriented. Dexter knew that the man was more interested in what time his auditors arrived for work than he did about their performance on audits. As long as paper flowed, innocuous and impotent, in and out of the department, he would be content. His first job upon arriving in his Chief Auditor position was to revise the department policy manual. The man sent a flurry of office memos—they flew from his suite like a flock of pigeons: harmless yet completely annoying—covering a range of subjects: vacation scheduling procedures, proper format for memoranda, sickness and absentee policy, instructions on ordering airline tickets, how much to spend on hotel accommodations, how much time to allow for lunch. The man's obsession with and propensity for inner-office correspondence was the reason Dexter knew that Ernie Gastineau was leaving on Friday at noon for a half-day of personal business.

He would wait for the waddler to leave before confronting Tula with the released memos—and her extracurricular duties. Dexter crouched behind the bank of cabinets, retrieving files, waiting to make his attack. He saw Ernie leave his office, lock the door, and check out with her. "Have a nice weekend, Tula," he said, and shuffled off. Dexter decided to wait a few minutes before springing. He consulted his watch and when exactly three minutes had passed, he peeked over the top.

Gastineau had disappeared.

Dexter took a step.

Tula picked up the telephone.

Dexter stopped, ducked down.

"Hi," she said. "Feeling any better?" There was a period of silence; he heard an occasional *uh huh, sure, I know*. And finally: "Mother we've been through this already." More pauses, more *uh huhs*, and then: "I can't do that, Mother. I still have ten years before I can retire. You'll make friends and I'll be there two or three times a week for dinner and you'll come home weekends. If you—"

When one of the other auditors walked past, Dexter glanced down at the open file folder. The man went by without looking over and continued on past Tula's desk, who wasn't talking now. She wasn't even making *uh huh* noises. "That's not fair, Mother," she suddenly blurted. "Look, I've got to go; I'll see you at home. We can talk about it then. Goodbye, Mother. I—"

He heard the receiver being replaced in its cradle, and stood. Still holding the file folder, he took a step backwards from the cabinets and then stopped. He waited for awhile longer before stepping into the open area; Tula sat hunched motionless over her desk. The offices were carpeted with an industrial-grade material and he took care not to make noise as he moved. Tula held her head in her hands. He watched, then turned toward his own office.

"Dexter," said the boy. "I've been looking for you. I wanted to thank you for the tip on the Houston audit."

Dexter looked at him, smiled quickly, and then looked in Tula's direction. She had turned in her chair and peered directly at him. Mascara streaked her cheeks. "Tell me about it," said Dexter.

"They weren't getting competitive bids for the refinery expansion and—"

Dexter put his hand on the young auditor's shoulder. "Give me a minute. I'll stop by your office."

The boy nodded and walked off past Tula's desk and into his cubicle by the north windows. Dexter went to her desk, file folder in hand. Tula blotted her eyes with tissue and looked up at him. He extended the folder. "These are Ernie's copies. He circled the typos. Let's reissue after corrections—for the record." She accepted the folder without comment, put it down next to her in-basket.

Dexter started toward the boy's cubicle, and was a few steps away when Tula spoke. "He doesn't have much of a backbone, does he?"

Dexter turned. "Really," he said. "Is he a man or a mollusk?"

She smiled, and Dexter turned to leave. The boy was on his telephone and gestured toward the single chair reserved for visitors. Dexter sat and twisted to look out the window. From here he could see the sprawl of apartment and office buildings to the north and west. He could see the Chicago River and the shoreline of Lake Michigan. He could see the armory and part of the lakeshore campus of Loyola University. He could see the running track and grassy area in the center and, just beyond, the complex of structures comprising Northwestern Hospital, where his own mother had spent her final hours more than two years ago.

Part Of The Process

On the morning of the day of his sister's arrival, Dexter Giles went for a bicycle ride in Lincoln Park. It had taken a crisis—their mother's stroke— to convince Delia to make the trip from California. Ten years of her excuses ran through his head: *I just can't get on an airplane and you know why. The boys aren't old enough to stay home by themselves. Larry has been out of town almost constantly this year. I can't leave until the addition is done.* And then she would finish with: *I sent Mother a real pretty nightgown. Why don't you bring her out here for Christmas? Did you get the birthday card from the boys?*

Dexter cycled through the zoo without seeing one animal. It was too early, or late, for them to be up. And he steered aimlessly left and right and arrived at the pedestrian bridge that spanned Lake Shore Drive without having ever consciously considered any specific destination. Two years ago he had resolved not to visit Delia again until she made the effort to come east. The fact that their mother hadn't wanted to make the trip for a year now hadn't had an impact. Delia had remained, entrenched in her four-bedroom Glendale house with her deferential husband, two spirited but spoiled children, and an Irish setter so stupid it didn't seek shelter in the rain.

In the middle of the bridge he leaned the bike on the railing and watched the traffic slip under him on the drive. It was misting hard enough to prevent him from seeing the lake, but the Sunday flow of cars was light enough to enable him to hear the chop of waves against the shore. He hadn't meant to yell at his sister. It was bad enough to fight face to face, but over the phone made it more difficult to work things out, though ultimately they'd both said they were sorry. But he knew from her tone she felt backed into a corner. Both had inherited a large measure of their mother's intransigence.

He looked at his watch and slumped over the railing. He removed his glasses, held his face in his hands, and rubbed vigorously. In a week he'd be leaving for Trinidad, to audit Imperial's oil production operations. That didn't leave much time for the arrangements. Dexter had broken a sweat despite the chill. For a time, in his forties, people occasionally told him he was handsome, and he had scoffed. He saw neatness and tidiness in his bathroom mirror, not attractiveness. Now that he was nearly sixty such comments never came his way. And recently his weight was up and his stomach had grown larger, in spite of the excursions on his new bicycle and his attempts to avoid red meat. For a month he'd been smoking cigarettes again.

***

As a boy, Dexter had been drawn to trains and train stations. Stations with granite interior columns, terrazzo floors, and broad sweeping staircases. In the hours spent watching trains in the switching yard, he'd once seen a five-wheel steam locomotive speed past on the B&O tracks. Most of the other boys his age seemed more interested in the jets that they were beginning to use for commercial flights, but Dexter had mourned even then for the world being left behind. Who wouldn't prefer the civility of a linen tablecloth and napkins in a clean, warm dining car over the indignity of a box lunch dropped onto a plastic tray smaller than a child's high-chair?

The new Union Station was a steel and glass monstrosity—more suited to the lobby of an insurance headquarters than a transportation terminus. Dexter consulted the *Arrivals* section of the Amtrak monitor and then headed for the platforms, and he spotted Delia almost immediately, up ahead through a break in the crowd. She had gained more weight. They approached each other cautiously. She smiled and then he smiled. Her complexion was healthy-looking, sanguine. She stood behind the push cart, which held her luggage, and made no move to step out in front.

"You look well-rested," said Dexter.

"I slept good on the train," said Delia. "I didn't get up until after eight. At home I'm up way before Larry and the boys. How's Mom?"

Dexter moved to take the luggage cart from her. She seemed reluctant at first to release it to him; her hands gripped the metal bar, but at least he didn't have to pry it from her fingers. He pushed the luggage in the direction of the exit, and Delia took her purse from the top of her biggest suitcase and draped it over her shoulder and they walked side by side for a minute or two in silence.

"We can probably take her home tomorrow or the next day. The doctor thinks it was a cerebral embolus, not a cerebral hemorrhage," said Dexter. Delia screwed her face. "Her stroke wasn't caused by a clot in the brain," said Dexter. "Her speech isn't slurred anymore and she gets up to go to the bathroom. How long can you stay?"

They were at the revolving doors, and so gathered the bags in their arms and abandoned the cart. Outside, in the chilled, spring air, a gust billowed Delia's coat around her, making her momentarily gigantic. She held a suitcase and her oversized purse and lurched as if she might lose her footing in the midst of the turbulence. Two boys, whom Dexter judged to be in their early teens, were sitting on a ledge that surrounded the plaza landscaping, and he watched as they looked at Delia and laughed. Dexter set his jaw and stared back at them until one of them whispered something to the other and the two averted their eyes.

"This is ridiculous," said Delia. "It's already May. I must say I don't miss this weather.

"A week. My return reservation is for next Saturday."

Dexter was thinking about the boys. The one with dark curls and rosy cheeks was beautiful, but the other was eventually going to be bigger than Delia if he didn't get off his fat ass and get some exercise. He stopped suddenly and looked at his sister. "That's not a week. That's six days."

"Larry has to go out of town a week from Wednesday."

"Fine."

Instead of walking toward the line of waiting taxis Dexter turned left and headed in the direction of the subway on State Street. "I'll pay for a cab," said Delia, who had plenty of experience with her brother's providence.

They made the ride north on Halsted. Neither a question about Dexter's life nor their Mother's health—after his initial briefing—did Delia ask. She talked about Mark and Taylor and her attempts to make sure that they got in the special advanced programs at school. "Larry and I want them in good colleges," she said. She recited test scores; she recounted the meetings held with reluctant teachers and not-convinced administrators; she detailed her attempts to prod the boys to study harder. And then she complained about Larry's frequent business trips.

The taxi lurched up Halsted Street. It had been a hard winter, leaving behind more potholes than paved road surface. They turned west on Armitage and north onto Magnolia, and Delia ducked her head down to look out at the houses. They stopped near the end of the block in front of Dexter's brick, two-storey house. "The tulips Mom gave you are coming up," said Delia. And then, "You changed the color of the trim." She opened her purse and took out a small wallet and, after thumbing through the bills for a moment, she pulled out a twenty and handed it to the driver. After accepting the change—a wad of singles—she counted out four to give back to the driver, but Dexter put his hand on her wrist as she stretched forward and shook his head. She looked at her brother and mouthed, *How much?*, and he indicated with three extended fingers.

Inside the front door Dexter deposited Delia's bags at the foot of the stairs. "I'll take those up; don't touch them," he said. He untied his shoes and deposited them on the shoe rack against the wall. Delia stepped out of her shoes too, and took off her coat and draped it over her arm.

"I'll just take this one," she said. With a grunt, she lifted the largest piece, canvas with a pink floral print, and started up the stairs, one at a time, in her stockinged feet. The stairways in these old row houses were narrow and this one barely accommodated the engorged suitcase and Delia's chunky hips. Dexter watched her struggle up the first few steps with a mixture of amusement and anger. "After you have your stroke, we'll see if we can't get you the bed next to Mother's," he said. Delia ignored him.

He walked through the living and dining rooms to the kitchen. He heard Debit and Credit meowing at the back door. He let them in and watched as they rushed to their food bowls. He took coffee from the freezer and filled the grinder with beans. He poured the finely ground powder into the basket and then sprinkled cinnamon on the top. After he had filled the pot with water and turned on the cof-fee-maker, he took down two cups.

***

When they entered their mother's room, she was star-ing at a crossword puzzle in the newspaper. Neither did she have a pen or a pencil in her hand, nor did Dexter see one on the tray table at the bedside.

"Well, how long you two been standing there?" said the woman.

Delia went over to the bed and bent down to kiss her mother, then straightened and looked at her brother. "She doesn't look bad at all," said Delia, as if the woman were not present in the room. "Her color is good."

"Yes, she's a lovely shade of gray," said Dexter. "Don't flatter her to the point where she'll ignore what has hap-pened. She has to have some respect for her health."

Delia sat in the chair next to the bed.

"Did you remember to water my plants, Dexter?" said his mother, looking at him. He stood at the foot of the bed, studying her chart, and she waited till he nodded before turning her attention back to her daughter. "How are the boys?"

"I'm going to look for the doctor," said Dexter. He walked down the corridor to the nurses' station. At the counter he stood, waiting for someone to acknowledge him. Even for a Sunday evening the hospital seemed quiet. The urgency that marked the other days of the week was not apparent. One would think that all days were alike when it came to sickness and disease. But people still seemed to consider the calendar when it came to matters of health. Or maybe the sick and dying were forced to wait for attention until some doctor finished his weekend of golf. Then Dexter remembered the colon examination he'd undergone just after Christmas. Lying on his side, covered by a waxy paper sheet, he'd glanced over his shoulder at the doctor while the man probed his bowels with rubber tubing. The overhead lights were out, but the physician's face was lit by weak light emitted from the goggle-like apparatus at the end of the hose that he was peering into. Dexter felt a jab of pain from time to time as the hose pressed against the wall of his intestine.

"You did a nice job of cleaning yourself out," said the doctor.

"Yes, I'm very anal," said Dexter.

He rapped twice on the countertop with his knuckles. "Excuse me, but what time is the doctor making rounds? I need to speak to him about Mrs. Giles in room 615."

*   *   *

Delia didn't have jet lag and wanted to go out to eat, but Dexter didn't want to sit in a crowded restaurant and listen to some way-too-enthusiastic waiter recite the day's specials. They agreed on the BAR Association down at the end of the block on the corner. A good compromise: there were less than six people in the whole restaurant. Dexter and Delia were seated at the table directly in front of the fireplace. Dexter sipped his scotch, leaned back in his chair, and stared into the flames. Delia sipped a martini. When the waiter placed menus on the table, she set down her glass and picked up the menus. She offered one to Dexter, and he shook his head. "I know what I want," he said.

"Are the pork chops still good?" said Delia.

"They're large," said Dexter.

"And?"

"Overcooked."

Delia studied the menu for a while longer. "What about the trout?" she said.

"Frozen," said Dexter.

"Shrimp?"

"Tough and gritty."

Delia slapped her menu shut and let out a sigh. "What are you having?"

"The burger. They use lean meat—I think it's beef—and if you order it rare they'll bring it out slightly pink."

"Sounds good," said Delia. She plucked one of the two olives from her glass with her thumb and forefinger, placed it in her mouth, and blotted her lips with her napkin. "I thought Mother looked pretty good," she said again, chewing the olive and spreading the cloth back across her lap.

Dexter took a cigarette from an inside pocket of his jacket and put it between his lips, then he placed it in the clean ashtray without having lit it. "She isn't going to be able to stay at home," said Dexter.

Delia looked at the cigarette in the ashtray. "I thought you quit."

"We must discuss the options," said Dexter. He'd spent considerable time lately, pondering them. He'd been the one to take care of their mother for years now, ever since Delia and Larry moved away. When he went overseas on assignments for a month or two at a time, she had fended for herself. All that was different now.

"Can't we get a home health-care worker?" said Delia.

"Where would the money come from? Part-time isn't good enough."

"Mother could come home with me for a month then come back and stay with you for a month. By then maybe she'll be able to go back home."

"Mother is eighty-four years old, Delia. The doctor says she's not out of the woods yet." Dexter took a roll from the basket and tore it in half. "And If I hear you gush about her color one more time—"

"So we'll put her in a home. That what you want to hear?"

Dexter had bread in his left hand, a knife in his right, and was poised over the butter. He put down the bread and knife and reached for the cigarette in the ashtray and lit it. "It's not what she wants to hear," he said.

***

Dexter made coffee, but resolved to wait to unload the dishwasher until Delia got up. Last night he'd been prepared for an argument at the restaurant and didn't know now whether to be relieved or disappointed. He heard Delia walking around upstairs and a few minutes later she appeared in the kitchen.

She smiled, asked Dexter how he had slept, and went to the coffee pot to pour herself a cup. "Do you hear from Jean Paul these days?" she said.

"He was a handful," said Dexter.

"You've been living alone for a long time now," said Delia.

"He sent a card from Amsterdam," said Dexter. He wet a sponge under the faucet and reached behind Delia to wipe the counter area around the coffee pot where she had spilled some. "I'm supposed to leave for Trinidad in a week. I could put it back a week if you can stay a little longer."

"I can't."

"A week isn't going to be enough time to find a facility."

"I can't."

When Delia was in first grade she'd been such a small thing, not half even the size of the other girls her age. One time their mother locked her out of the house early in the morning: a disagreement over a nickel for milk at school. Delia cried, threw a tantrum really. The money, usually collected on Wednesday, was due on Tuesday. Delia was a willful child, not above conniving for a little spare change and who could blame their mother for having not believed her. It was Delia who found all the presents, long before Christmas day, opened them, examined them, and sealed them shut before anyone but Dexter was the wiser. Some of the seams were askew and the tape came unstuck. Their mother had literally pushed her out the door that day and locked it. Delia ran from the front yard to the back, crying and pounding on the doors and windows to get in. "Mrs. Frank told us to bring our money today," she screamed, again and again. Dexter felt a pang for his little sister but may have simply been relieved to not be the focus of the stressed woman's abuse. Then there had been the sound of glass shattering and Delia's hysterics. She had cut her hand on the pane in the door. It wasn't a serious wound, but there had been a lot of blood.

"I called Larry last night," said Delia. "He's going to arrange for a meeting with the principal at Bishop. I'm just furious. Taylor's teacher didn't recommend him for the advanced curriculum next year."

"Isn't Taylor the one who flunked kindergarten?" said Dexter.

"He didn't flunk. He's shy. And he didn't like his teacher. You should see the one he has now. She a big butch thing with huge shoulders and chopped-off greasy hair." Delia opened the cupboards and peered inside. "You have flour and sugar," she said. She pushed a few items to the side, shifted others to the front. "And cinnamon and baking powder," she said. "Do you have any pecans? I'll make sticky buns." Dexter opened the freezer door and took out a package of nuts and dropped them on the counter. Delia had moved over to the cabinets above the sink. "Can you reach that mixing bowl?" She sifted flour and poured sugar. She peeled foil from the butter, opened the cellophane, and measured the nuts. The air was clouded with flour dust. Delia attended to matters of food with the urgency of an addict. "Taylor's test scores were more than adequate for the advanced program. This is personal." Delia had the bowl cradled in her arm and was stirring vigorously with a wooden spoon. "If Larry has trouble setting up the meeting I may have to leave a day or two early," she said.

Dexter had taken off his glasses and was pinching the bridge of his nose. He put them back on and stared at Delia, as if to read his sister's thoughts, and said, "Delia, what in Heaven is wrong with you? Mother had a stroke, and I need some help."

"I'm sorry, Dexter, but my children come first."

"I fail to see that by helping your mother you're depriving your children. Someday you may need them. How would you like it if they turned their backs on you?"

"They won't. I don't treat them like Mother treated me. She didn't treat you like she treated me."

***

Dexter and Delia's father, Tilghman Giles, had been a practical man. At one time Dexter thought he knew a lot about his deceased father, but he realized now that he had possessed a few simple statistics and nothing more. The man, who died of a ruptured appendix when Dexter was thirteen—and Delia was six—had traveled throughout the Tri-State area in a brown Chevrolet coupe peddling life insurance, and if nothing more, his enthusiasm for his product line had left his widow, Eulalia, financially self-sufficient. But his early and untimely death had also left her somewhat bitter, though not because she was lonely. She had grown more accustomed to her husband's absences than his occasional week or two at home, when he poked from room to room like a stranger in their three-bedroom bungalow on Chicago's northwest side, and for years after his passing Eulalia Giles had to remind herself that he wasn't simply driving through some remote, green town in Wisconsin. She was resentful because, at forty-one, she found herself in the position of having allowed Tilghman Giles to neglect her, and their children, on the promise of a richer and fuller tomorrow—a tomorrow that regretfully had failed to materialize.

Together Delia and Dexter had managed to get their mother, in wheelchair, up the seven front steps onto her porch and then into the house. Dexter had pulled from the back and Delia had pushed from the front, turning the wheels backwards with her hands. "Let me walk," said their mother, "before you both end up in wheelchairs."

In the front room the old woman stood and tottered to her beige-colored recliner, the chair Dexter found her in the night he stopped in after work. He had stepped through the front door and recognized at once the odor of burning meat. He turned on the lights, saw his mother stretched out in the chair. "Why are you sitting in the dark?" he said. She blinked, but Dexter rushed to the kitchen before she had a chance to reply. An aluminum pan, with a charcoal-like chunk of pot roast, smoldered on the stove, but the exhaust fan, on high, was sucking most of the smoke out of the house. Dexter speared the charred remains and discarded it, then turned off the burner and took the pot to the sink to hold it under the faucet. Water ricochetted off of the metal in furious beads. Back in the living room he stood over his mother. "Turned on me," she said, barely moving her lips. "Turned on me." Dexter sniffed the air and stepped in close and that was when he identified the acrid and humiliating odor of his mother's urine.

"Oh, I left the chicken in the car," said Delia. "I'll go get it." She opened the front door, then turned to look at Dexter. He had taken an afghan off the back of the sofa and was arranging it across their mother's lap. "Do we want to eat in the living room?" said Delia. "*Dynasty* is on tonight. I could dish up everything and put it on the coffee table."

"I don't like eating and watching television," said their mother.

"Must your every thought center on the preparation, display, and consumption of food?" said Dexter.

"I'm just trying to help," said Delia. She went through the door and slammed it behind her. When she came back inside with the boxed chicken, she stomped to the kitchen. Dexter glanced at his watch, then at his mother, and walked to the kitchen after her.

Delia opened the paper sacks, removed the containers of potatoes, slaw, and gravy, and aligned them on the Formica countertop. One by one she removed the plastic lids, then she put her forefinger in the gravy and tasted it. Dexter stood just behind Delia and put his hand on her thick shoulder. "I'll bring the portable TV in from Mother's bedroom and put it here on the counter," he said. He started to leave to retrieve the television, but stopped at the door when Delia started to speak.

"Sometimes, I hate coming back," she said. "It feels like I'm seven years old again. I try to imagine being in this house every day for sixty years and it nearly drives me crazy. The same corny pictures on the walls, the same musty carpets, the same yellowed appliances, the same lumpy mattresses." Delia looked out through the back window to the yard. Dexter was still standing in the doorway. "The same gray weather day after day and no place to escape it."

"Is this going to be one of your California sales pitches again?" said Dexter, smiling. "If it is, spare me."

"At least you've seen the world. She's never gone anywhere. She has no life."

"She enjoys her grandchildren," said Dexter.

"Remember how she acted when I was pregnant with Mark?" Delia looked up from the food. A clump of her hair had fallen down in her face; she brushed it back with her fingers. Her lower lip trembled. "She told me to stay in the bedroom when Mrs. Warburg came to the front door. She said I was showing too much to have only been married four months and that Mrs. Warburg would think it was a shotgun wedding. The whole time I was pregnant she was an old grouch."

"She was always excited to be going out to visit you.

"And things were fine for a few days. Then she'd get into one of her moods and get everyone else in one too. Taylor cried after they lost their big soccer game and all she said was, 'Well, what's he crying about?' She has no sympathy for anyone."

Dexter walked over to the round, maple table and pulled out a chair and sat down. "Delia, I've lived with Mother's disapproval for years. I'm still living with it. I just don't dwell on it." Then their mother appeared behind Delia in the doorway.

"Are we going to eat?" she said. Dexter stood and watched as Delia turned and hurried over to her.

"We were just coming to get you," said Delia. She took their mother by the arm, led her to the table, and helped her into a chair. As Delia squeezed back past Dexter to get the food, she looked at him with pursed lips and raised eyebrows. Dexter shrugged.

He looked down at his mother's boney shoulders and thinning hair. She had her hands clasped together in her lap and was staring vacantly out the back window. Who had ever known, even in healthy times, what the woman was really thinking? "I'll set the table," said Dexter.

***

At his office, on the twenty-third floor of Imperial's marble-clad headquarters, Dexter had spent most of the morning on the telephone. One facility, Berkshire Gardens, on Chicago's north side, stressed: *Beautiful, spacious gardens and grounds.* Another, Lakeview Convalescent Center, boasted: *Sixty-one percent of our patients in a recent quarter went home happy and healthy.* A third claimed: *A special place for special people.* Dexter had circled one particularly unctuous advertisement in the yellow pages: *Faced with the difficult decision of placing a loved one in a nursing home? We care! We are the best! Let us help!*

He was about to contact the insurance company when his telephone rang, two short, quick rings, signaling an outside call. He picked up the receiver. "Dexter Giles," he said. There was a pause—and the muffled sound of conversation—before Delia came on the line. Then the audible sound of her chewing as she spoke: "I started a diet this morning."

"So I hear," said Dexter. "How's Mother?"

"Don't be a bitch; it's cottage cheese and pineapple. She's fine. How's it on your end?"

"You're in a good mood this morning," said Dexter.

"Mother is sleeping," said Delia. "And I have some good news for you too. I talked to Larry this morning. I can stay another week."

Dexter looked at the clutter of paper on his desk. He checked his calendar, counted the days till Trinidad. "Good," he said. "We'll need to confront Mother with dispatch." He flipped through the pages of his Daily Planner. "How's four o'clock, Friday? I'll leave work early."

Delia laughed. "I'll tell my secretary to pencil it in. Don't you want to know why I can stay longer?" she said.

***

Ever since their choice of Friday, Dexter had run through the various ways of breaking the news to their mother. And he had tried to imagine her reaction. Ultimately he had concluded, after a discussion with Delia, that there wasn't enough time to get the woman enrolled and moved before he left for his audit and Delia left for California. They decided—rather Dexter decided and Delia went along—to get temporary home care until he returned from the Caribbean. Dexter descended the stairs from the El platform and exited through the turnstile. It was an hour till the rush hour and there were only a few riders in the station. He rounded the corner and walked north on Whipple, a street that had reflected few changes over the years. The sunshine and warm air bolstered his resolve. He removed his topcoat, draped it over his arm, and began to hum "The Colonel Bogie March." A full-care facility was ultimately the only real option. Somehow in Chicago one appreciated a nice day so much more. Mild weather was never taken for granted. The trees were leafing out still greener and some of the neighbors had planted summer flowers in their yards. Still, doing the right thing was seldom easy. He felt an unanticipated urge to cry. He could hide there, under Mrs. Warburg's porch, and sob for as long as he wanted, just as he had done as a child of ten. Of course, Mrs. Warburg hadn't lived there for several years. Regrettably, she had died of throat cancer, and not the news of Delia's *untimely* pregnancy. What did that amount to now? What did any of it amount to? Their mother had spent her life taking care of her children. And now they couldn't—

He chased the thought from his head and quickened his pace when his mother's house came into view. He bounded up the steps of the porch. Recently, on Fridays, he'd been stopping in at The Earl for an end-of-the-week drink before going home. Unlike Jean Paul, he never left with any of the boys, who leaned, slouched, and flexed at stations around the bar, but he did enjoy watching the other old men jostle and elbow their way to the entrance whenever a *hot number* came in off the street. Dexter entered and smelled the aroma of roasting chicken and rosemary. In the kitchen,

Delia smiled at him. "Mother's on the porch," said his sister. "She wanted to sit outside."

"Let's go," said Dexter.

"Before dinner?" said Delia.

Dexter removed his suit jacket, hung it on the back of his chair at the table, and loosened his tie. He opened the aluminum storm door and stepped onto the porch. His mother smiled at him too. He moved closer and patted her on the shoulder. Delia sat down in the empty chair, next to their mother; Dexter leaned against the porch's wooden railing in front of her. He was about to utter some banality about the weather when the old woman said, "Don't you leave for Trinidad and Tobago on Sunday?"

He glanced at Delia, and she shook her head. "I've put it off a week," he said.

"And I'm staying another week, Mother," said Delia. "So that—"

"I feel like such a burden," said their mother. She clenched her hands into frail fists and put them up to her eyes.

As a younger man Dexter had feared death. Now he feared the prospect of too long a life and the possibility of a slow, painful death. Perhaps his own father had been lucky, struck down as he had been, at an early age, without any warning. And at least his mother would have him nearby, to stop in from time to time for a surprise audit; at least he would be able to show them at the home that he wouldn't tolerate the mistreatment of his mother. And who would there be for him? Who would stop them from cramming pills down his mouth, or slapping him when his mashed peas dribbled down his chin, or abandoning him for days on end in his wheelchair in a sterile, darkened room without the possibility of Mozart or Mahler? And what made Delia think she'd fare any better? She moved to California and left her family. Wait till her little geniuses moved their families to Brussels and Tokyo.

"You're not a burden, Mother," said Dexter. For a moment he couldn't go on. There was such a silence that he could hear the sound of his own eyelashes. "But," he said, "Delia and I don't think you should live alone any more."

The old woman looked up at him. "You could sell your house. This is going to be yours anyway someday," she said to Dexter. "And yours too, Delia. "You can move back home, Dexter." She stared, first at him and then at Delia, as if the force of her will were enough. "But that's not what you mean, is it?" she said, when Dexter turned away to remove his glasses and rub his eyes.

"I don't want to sell my house. We want to bring someone in to take care of you until—"

"Cause I have to go home, Mother. I can only stay another week. And Dexter has his business trip—" Dexter scowled at Delia to silence her.

"I've been talking to nursing services and I've—we've—narrowed it down to three. They're coming by tomorrow so you can meet them and make a choice. Choose the one you get along with best." From audits, Dexter knew the value in making others part of the process.

"You mean to come in during the days?" she said.

"And nights too. She'll, or he'll, there's one young man, live here. And when I get back in two months we can visit some nice retirement homes. We'll pick one you like."

"Is he a friend of yours?" said their mother.

"Who?" said Dexter. Delia covered a smile with the back of her hand.

"The young man," said their mother, through tight lips.

Dexter felt the color rise in his face. "I've only talked to these people on the telephone. It will be your choice."

Delia leaned away from her mother's chair, but Dexter hovered over her as if prepared to return a serve. Both Dexter and Delia watched and waited. But Mrs. Giles didn't speak or move; she stared out into the yard. Then she yawned. A yawn so pronounced, so full of gums and yellow teeth, that it must have taken all her strength to endure it.

***

Dexter and Delia had eaten their chicken and vegetables without their mother, after numerous attempts to get her to leave her bed and come to the table. They decided at last to ignore her. "I say we just leave her in there and go down to the Wand. A drag show will cheer us up," said Delia. Instead they spent the evening in the living room of their mother's house. Dexter walked to the liquor store, a few blocks over, and brought back two bottles of red Bordeaux and they settled at opposite ends of the sofa to discuss life and remember old times. Dexter admitted to his sister that he was lonely and he confided that he was angry that she hadn't made more of an effort to come home on a regular basis. For her part Delia told him she'd always been a failure here and that she had a chance now to be a success—with her own children. At the end of the evening, after they had finished both bottles, Dexter stubbed out a cigarette, stood, and said: "I've got to go home and feed the cats. I'll be by in the morning." Then he hugged his sister.

On Saturday their mother came out of her bedroom, but she refused to look at or speak to either of them. And she didn't participate in the interviews of the home health-care workers. Ultimately Dexter and Delia chose the middle-aged woman, Carol, who walked with a limp; she said she could start on Thursday. The other woman refused to smile and continued to stress, long after Dexter said he understood, that she would not be coming in to do housework. The young man seemed to have the rosiest disposition, but the only time during the three interviews when their mother showed the slightest interest in anyone was when the tall, thin boy asked if Mrs. Giles liked animals. She glared at him through rheumy eyes while he described in curious detail the antics of his miniature Schnauzers, both of which he said were waiting outside in the car, and: "Would anyone like to meet them?"

There never was an opportunity for Dexter or Delia to determine if they had made the right choice. Delia called Dexter at the office on Tuesday, early in the afternoon. Dexter had just returned from a luncheon of chow mein with the new Staff Auditor from Michigan. Though it was uncharacteristic of Dexter to discuss personal problems with those at work, there was something about the boy's grin and the way he leaned in close when Dexter spoke that made him wish to disclose his feelings. Discussing the details of his mother's situation had helped—until Delia called.

"She didn't come out at breakfast. And I fried sausage and made homemade biscuits and gravy. She hasn't come out for lunch either," said Delia.

"Did you go in and check on her?" said Dexter.

"I think maybe the door is locked," said Delia.

"You must have burned the biscuits," said Dexter. He lit a cigarette and waited.

Their mother hadn't been effusive on Sunday and Monday, but at least the woman had answered when he or Delia addressed her. He knew even before she came back to the phone. "My God, Lizzie," he said, "why didn't you use an axe?" In the hospital lobby, he spoke at length with the doctor. The diffused light from outside illuminated the man's blue eyes with intensity. His lips and jaw worked methodically as he held his final conference regarding the patient, but Dexter saw a mouth that sulked whenever challenged. "Mrs. Giles suffered another stroke, probably during the night or early this morning. Perhaps if we'd gotten her here earlier we could have done something," said the man. Delia cried for the first time, sitting in the lounge, her hands locked onto the box of tissue in her lap. "She's barely breathing, Dexter; I think she's unconscious." Afterwards, Delia refused to go back to their mother's house.

She went to Dexter's. He returned, just to check on things, and agreed to bring back her overnight case.

Darkness still came early in May. And with it this evening a cold and windy rain. Dexter walked under the canopy, from the revolving door of Northwestern Hospital to the street and the line of waiting taxis. On Lake Shore Drive he glanced out the back window of the cab at the Imperial Petroleum Building. The lower floors were lit but the upper floors were obscured by the sweep of rain swirling off the lake. In spite of his cautionary remarks to Delia he hadn't had time to prepare for his mother's death. He had already imagined entering her room at the home with sunflowers and a carved talisman of ivory, a gift from his travels to some exotic, foreign land. He could almost feel the warmth of her smile.

He stood in the heavy rain, his umbrella unopened at his side, and watched the receding taillights of the taxi as it drove into the distance. When it rounded the corner and he could no longer see the two dots of glowing red, he turned and looked at her house. It seemed impossible that she had filled the rooms with such energy, and he ached for an answer as to where all that intensity had gone.

The living room floor creaked familiarly under Dexter's feet. He had convinced her to let him paint this room and the dining room a year ago, but she had steadfastly refused to get new carpeting. He went into her bedroom, just off the dining room, and turned on the lamp on her dressing table.

He sat on the edge of her unmade bed and clasped his hands together in his lap. Then he reached down, picked up a clump of lint and dust from the rug, and worked it into a small ball with his fingers. At the edge of the night table, on the floor, he picked up several large crumbs too, and he placed them in the palm of his left hand to examine them. The hardened chunks of biscuit had dropped from Delia's hand as she hovered over the bed, eating and watching as their mother died. How many hours did the woman lie there, struggling for air and blood? Surely the contorted flesh of her face must have betrayed her rigid suffering.

He stood and walked over to her dressing table. The metallic-gold music box that his father had given to their mother on the occasion of their anniversary one year was on the surface of the table in the precise spot where it had been for as long as Dexter could remember. The music box, round and bell-shaped, had a faded painting of red and yellow roses on the lid. He turned the box over, wound it, and placed it upright again on the dressing table. Then he removed the lid and listened to the measured mechanical tinkling of "William Tell's Prayer."

He was ten again, no stranger to life's sadness, but he felt safe in his mother's room, with the combined scents of her powders and perfumes drifting on unseen currents. She was in the kitchen cooking; Delia was asleep in her crib at the foot of the bed; and his father would be coming home for supper any time now.

Technicalities

Under the scrutiny of those at nearby tables, Dexter
Giles read the financial section; he completed the
crossword puzzle, wrote a letter to his sister, and
pencilled the beginnings of a grocery list; he swallowed
three cups of lifeless coffee and six glasses of water; he ate
all but the last muffin from an entire basketful, while the
waitress no longer bothered to smile when she stopped by
to see if he wished finally to order. Antonio was late for
dinner by nearly an hour, and Dexter began to consider the
possibility, with progressing irritation, that his spoiled for-
mer-friend wouldn't show.

He peered out through the plate glass window. Until
the telephone call, Dexter had believed he might never see
him again. Most of the time, he succeeded in not thinking
about Antonio and he dismissed his desire for revenge now
as an unhealthy preoccupation. After Antonio called, Dexter pictured himself pulling up in front of the restaurant in
his new car; he rehearsed how he would mention his condominium overlooking Lincoln Park; he planned the way he
would describe his life in retirement; he practiced smiling
until his jaw ached to belie any hint of his bitterness. A
performance quite justified after all: Antonio had arranged
this meeting no doubt because he needed a favor: a loan or
a place to stay.

He had decided to ask for his check when he saw the
yellow taxi. The driver idled at the curb for a long time, as
he might for a contentious passenger disputing the fare or
an arthritic passenger trying to extract his wallet from an
unyielding hip pocket. The young man—the baggy, surf-
ing-style cut of his clothing made him initially appear
young—struggled out of the back seat. His movements,
though, resembled those of an old man as he stepped onto
the sidewalk and turned stiffly to close the door.

Though he had seen Antonio briefly, over the years,
Dexter wasn't completely sure that it was Antonio who approached, entered the restaurant, and scanned the room.

And not just because he stood at the doorway lit on one side by the eerie, pale orange of the street and on the other by the stark fluorescence of the interior. Once, in the bars, men had turned to take another look and then stepped back to make room for his entry; strangers had stood watching while acquaintances pressed forward to stand close, to touch him, to laugh at his jokes, and yes to make sexually suggestive remarks that they hoped might be taken seriously. Now, he walked with a limp, his black curls had been chopped off, and he seemed short of breath.

Antonio approached Dexter's table and stood next to the empty chair. "You've lost weight," said Antonio.

Dexter smiled, and averted his eyes. "Yes, and inches at Gloria Marshall." Then he added, in a more serious tone, "I figured it wasn't too late to exercise." Antonio's angular frame and boney face startled him. How mean-spirited it was, to have judged him so harshly. Perhaps he merely wanted closure. At a time like this there was so much one might say, but Dexter Giles was like others in the way he treated the obviously-ill: he pretended not to notice. He stood, stepped forward, and gave him a hug. "I waited to order," he said.

Antonio's arms dangled as if he lacked the power to move them, and Dexter released him and studied his own hands as if he expected to find the imprint of protruding shoulder blades on his palms.

"Food disgusts me," said Antonio. He sat and stared around the room. Dexter sat again, in the opposing chair, spread his napkin across his lap, adjusted his silverware, and said: "Still living in Florida?" Except for the moment when Antonio first approached, he hadn't made eye contact, and he continued now to peer silently into the distance, so Dexter took the last muffin from the basket and spread jam on it, and repeated his question. Though Antonio failed to meet his gaze, he did reply: "I was too sick to work. I came home when I came down with MAC."

"And how is Natalie?" said Dexter.

Antonio looked at him now, his eyes open wide and darting as he scanned Dexter's face. "I'm having night sweats and fevers," said Antonio, "and she asks her minister to come pray for me. She says I'm going to Hell. I'm going back to Miami."

"Miami is Hell," said Dexter, smiling.

Antonio didn't smile back.

Natalie had always refused to give Dexter information regarding Antonio's whereabouts. Dexter insisted that he didn't hate Antonio's sister, but he found it necessary to conceal a blossoming smile when she told them that time that Wayne had left her and the boys.

In three weeks it would be Christmas. Outside, the Belmont light poles were draped with red-ribboned wreaths and Santa Claus heads, but the temperature had climbed into the fifties and the sun had managed to poke through the clouds. Antonio didn't have a hat, and though he wore a sweatshirt and jeans, he gave the impression of being cold, with his arms held close to his body.

AIDS and close-cropped hair went together; there wasn't the strength for grooming. Or the motivation. Once, Antonio had cluttered their vanity with hair-care products. Dexter sometimes stood in the bathroom doorway watching as he rubbed lotion on his hairless chest, as he smiled at his own reflection. "I put a pubie across the bottle cap," said Antonio. "Did you touch my finishing spray?"

Antonio hacked. A dry, unproductive cough. But Dexter didn't reach across the table to take his hand. He noticed now the sallow, septic cast of Antonio's complexion. "Come over? Stay with me for a few days?" said Dexter.

"Isn't this the old funeral home?" said Antonio.

"They expanded," said Dexter.

These days a person had to put his name on a list and wait for half an hour or more in line. Ordinarily Dexter wouldn't have bothered; the food wasn't that good anymore. In the seventies and eighties, it had been a one-room restaurant famous for its Swedish cooking and freshly-baked pies. A simpler time when too many men went casually from partner to partner and lover to lover.

"You're welcome to stay with me awhile," said Dexter again.

***

The sun disappeared behind the highrise buildings, a little after four, lowering the temperature by twenty degrees. The baseball cap that Antonio had taken from his backpack fit him loosely, resting at the tops of his ears. Dexter heard his teeth chatter, saw him shiver, but it was too dark in the taxi for him to tell if he was perspiring. Antonio, twenty years his junior, would be forty-eight at the end of October. But of course it was more than the difference in ages that had made their alliance a difficult one.

"Should we stop at Natalie's?" said Dexter, eying the canvas bag.

"I've got my drugs," said Antonio.

On the northeast corner of Sheridan and Diversey, Dexter looked at the two Mies van der Rohe buildings. Antonio had stayed in the one closest to the lake, with Joe, after the separation. For months, Dexter had looked away when he passed for fear of seeing Antonio in the glass-enclosed lobby.

At the entrance to Dexter's building, one could hear the cry of gulls over the lake, see the reflection of the sky's fading light on the surface of Diversey Harbor. But Antonio didn't notice. He walked into the building and through the lobby to the elevator deliberately, lifting each shoe, raising each leg, planting each foot so tediously that no one would have blamed him if he had stopped, right then and there, and refused ever after to take another step.

The telephone rang as Dexter pushed open the door to his apartment. He struggled with the key, trying to pull it from the lock, and wrestled with Antonio's bag, then took hold of his elbow. Antonio began to cough. Dexter ignored the phone and led Antonio down the brightly-lit hallway into the bedroom; perspiration dotted his forehead and upper lip, and he struggled harder for breath. As Dexter pulled down the spread, Antonio took two wobbly steps backwards and leaned against the wall; his shoulder hit the corner of a picture frame, knocking it askew.

"I'll sleep on the couch in my office," said Dexter. He straightened the painting, then took Antonio's arm and helped him to the bed. Dexter's new, yellow cat jumped from the floor up onto the pillow, and Antonio reached out to stroke its head. "Is this Debit or Credit?" said Antonio.

Dexter started to explain that his Abyssinians had died, within a month of each other, in the fall, but decided to avoid any reference to death. "This is CEO," he said. "He runs the place."

"I need towels to soak up my sweat," said Antonio. He looked at the armoire at the bed's foot. "I knew your new place would be nice." Then he looked toward the window. "You're pretty high up," he said.

"The bedroom is small, but all I do is sleep in here," said Dexter, thankful for the speck of conversation, though his disclosure, made without forethought, was not in keeping with the image of a contented, prosperous, and sexually-satisfied gay man—a man undaunted by the reality of old age—that he had hoped to present. He needn't have worried; it took all of Antonio's mental effort just to stay upright, and when Dexter saw that the comment had not suffered analysis (indeed Antonio seemed almost not to have heard it) Dexter went for the towels.

In the bathroom, he picked two faded blue and white striped ones from the shelf. He went back into the bedroom and spread them out on top of the sheets. He thought Antonio might need help undressing, but merely watched as he took off his sneakers and stood to unfasten his jeans. He continued to watch as Antonio unzipped and slid the pants over his hips and to his ankles, then, winded, sat on the bed without actually pulling them off. Antonio used to spend so much time at the gym, but his buttocks had all but disappeared. Dexter stooped to pull the jeans over his ankles and feet. "Is this your first infection?" he said.

Antonio nodded. "I only have seven T-cells," he said.

After helping him into gray cotton sweat pants and a fresh tee shirt and settling him in bed, Dexter went into the office and dialed his voice mail. He listened to the first two messages and then he heard her: "This is Natalie. He's there, isn't he?" Dexter pushed *three* and erased her.

He sat on the sofa and picked up his book, opened to the spot marked by the jacket flap, and stared at the page for a minute or two before putting the book back down. Unless one counted his platonic association with Jean Paul, Dexter had never had a long-term relationship—until he met Antonio. And even now, with all the years of distance, he still could not explain the attraction. Had he simply been addicted to the boy's blue eyes and vascular forearms? Their relationship had lasted a year, despite the abuse. Or possibly, as Jean Paul had pointed out, because of it.

***

Dexter didn't sleep through the night anymore. Restlessness (from heartburn and an insistent bladder), a gift that had accompanied him since his sixtieth birthday, eight years ago, kept him shuffling in and out of the bathroom. At 3:00 A.M., when he got up for an antacid tablet and to pee, he saw the light under the back bathroom door. He heard a screeching, or a howling, too. He went to the door and knocked, but got no response. After a muffled, "Oh, oh, oh," Dexter pushed open the door to find Antonio stooped over the toilet. He vomited a stream of orange liquid, raised up on his toes to take a breath, and hunched over again to release another stream. A liminal existence. He was more dead than alive. Dexter put his hand on Antonio's back; the tee shirt was soaked.

***

At 8:00 A.M. Dexter called his attorney to tell him that he wouldn't be able to make their appointment, then he entered the bedroom. It had been close to six in the morning before he'd been able to stretch out on the couch. He monitored Antonio's temperature, watching it fall gradually from 104 to 103 and 102; when it stabilized at 100 degrees, he left the bedroom and went into the office. He couldn't sleep though, and got up again and went to bring in the morning paper from the hallway, when he heard it hit the door.

Antonio couldn't take anything orally to reduce his fevers; he told Dexter that he had suppositories and asked him to get one from his bag and peel it out of its hard, foil shell. He had given himself an injection too. Atavan to ease the pain and then he had slept. The morning sun seeped through the slats of the blinds casting a vertical shadow of bars on the wall.

"Are you awake?" said Dexter. He sat softly on the edge of the bed and put his hand on Antonio's shoulder. Antonio was dry now but still hot. "I'm going to Natalie's. Do you need anything?"

"I'm comfortable," said Antonio, and though his lids fluttered he did not open his eyes. "I'll stay here in bed," he said.

Had the buzzing receded from its usual level of static? Were colorful, amorphous images flashing through his mind with such rapidity that he could not actually label them? Faces, smiling clay-mation faces, and animals, ferret-like and unthreatening? Dexter looked at the nightstand. There were now two empty vials, two alcohol swabs, and another syringe next to the lamp. Antonio had pretended to be asleep after Dexter left the bed and given himself a second shot. Not that Dexter would have stopped him; Antonio had usually gotten what he wanted in spite of Dexter's sensible and logical arguments. Maybe taking more was all that mattered, so that thoughts about the pain, breaking through again, could not register.

"Should I bring anything back?" said Dexter. An occasional sexual encounter to relieve tension would have been one thing, but the affairs that Antonio concealed until faced with evidence by an outraged Dexter, were quite another. Perhaps the cheating made him feel alive, gave him the illusion of control. Why did it matter if Antonio, like others, was attracted to Dexter because he wore Italian-cut suits and silk ties and had a BMW at a time when most people thought it was a British car?

"No, nothing," said Antonio.

***

He drove around Natalie's block three times before he found parking. Hers was a crowded neighborhood of six- and ten-unit buildings north of Wrigley Field that had changed little since he and Antonio had helped her move after Wayne left. Helping had been Antonio's idea: to give her some support during a hard time, he said. But it was a strained and uncomfortable day that made Dexter's back ache. Natalie regarded him with suspicion, even before Antonio told her that he was gay and that he and Dexter were more than friends, but it deteriorated into furtive glances of examination and outright hostility afterwards.

As Natalie opened the door, she looked immediately past him to the stairway. "Is he in the car?" she said.

"He's going to stay with me for the time being," said Dexter.

"I'll come and get him if I have to," said Natalie. She put her hand to her face, covering her mouth, and stood back from the door.

Dexter stepped inside. The acrid scent of rubbing alcohol penetrated his nostrils. In the far corner, video games and wrapped presents had been placed on the floor beneath a small tree, decorated with Christmas ornaments, candy canes, and colored lights. (And topped with a white angel.) A framed picture of Jesus (he had carted it from the truck and up the flight of stairs that day along with her other cheap, framed posters) occupied a centered position over the sofa, and despite the clutter, Dexter noticed, after he and Natalie sat down, a white Bible on the table and a pamphlet: *You Have A Friend In Jesus.*

As one looked around the room, what really caught the eye and held one's attention, what destroyed Natalie's attempt to create a holiday mood, was the I.V. stand decorated with tubing and clear plastic bags of medicine. Underneath this tree was a red container for used syringes and a red plastic bag for hazardous waste.

Natalie needed a friend. The swollen skin around her eyes was discolored, and when she wrung her hands he noticed that she still bit her nails till they bled.

"He took out his I.V. and he didn't do his TPN last night," she said. "He can't eat; he has to have TPN or he'll—" Natalie's voice broke and she looked down at her hands before continuing: "You have no idea what I do."

"I know you told him he was doomed," said Dexter. His hands shook. The words had lodged in his throat at first; the only way he got them out without shouting was by lowering his voice and speaking slowly. Still, he placed too much emphasis on the word doomed, and Natalie, who had been sitting forward on the edge of the sofa with her hands and arms in her lap, sat back and grabbed onto the doily-covered arm for support.

Dexter knew she read his anger by the deepened register of his voice. Despite his protestations years before, when Antonio had lived with him, about how he cared for her brother, supported him, paid all his bills, she no doubt still believed Dexter had corrupted Antonio—encouraged him to choose the path that he had.

Natalie took a breath and sat forward again. "Even you could have The Lord's forgiveness," she said.

Dexter stood. He faced Natalie, and started to reply, then decided simply to leave. He'd said what he had come to say. How absurd she was. Being a Christian meant that one was selfless not selfish. But it was beyond Natalie's ability to see that her motives for urging Antonio to eat, to fight, to take another mouthful were in her interest and not Antonio's. She stared at Dexter's chest. No doubt her pastor had told her that it was her Christian duty to make her brother see the error of his ways, told her that it was her responsibility to save him. Dexter pictured a cheerless man, gray eyes watering, skin taut and pink from vigorous scrubbing, in a private sermon outside Antonio's door, exhorting her to bring about a rebirth in her brother. *The road to Hell for us all is a paved, super highway; the road to Heaven is a narrow, tricky path.*

"I do his laundry, clean up his vomit, feed him pills by the hundred, lug him back and forth to the doctor," said Natalie, holding out her palms, as if to plead for understanding. "How can you allow him to leave."

She stared at him now, her face flushed, waiting for his reaction. A plastic container for urine and a box of disposable latex gloves were on the floor next to Natalie's feet. Dexter noticed too the underlying odors of vomit and excrement, emerging now, to overpower the smell of disinfectant. He peered at the latex gloves for a moment longer and then said: "So if I do those things for a week or two, it'll give you a break."

"He needs spiritual care too; I pray," said Natalie. "You can't help. You threw him out."

Resisting the urge to spew insults, Dexter stepped in haste to the door, and when he was a stride away, he turned to face her. Though her mouth was drawn tight and her jaw clenched, she seemed almost to smile, as if she thought she had delivered a blow which he could not deflect.

"I didn't come here to find salvation," said Dexter.

***

Antonio had not gotten out of bed. When Dexter tried to talk about Natalie, he only shrugged. "She has a point," said Dexter. "I don't know anything about—"

"I deserve to be comfortable. At least let me have a view of the lake." He glowered and hesitated, before continuing. "Don't worry, Dexter. I won't inconvenience you too much."

Antonio studied Dexter's impassive face and coughed.

"You didn't tell me about all your medication," said Dexter. "What is TPN?"

"A fucking feed-bag dinner," said Antonio. His coughing grew in intensity until he gagged, but this time he was spared the impulse to vomit. Dexter's lack of expression, his attempt to hide his concern, he knew, had always revealed it. Antonio possessed the ability to read his moods. When Dexter joked and laughed, Antonio pressed for favors: "Let me take your car; I'll be back early." When Dexter frowned and sorted mail, Antonio soothed and comforted: "We'll eat in more often, cut back on trips."

Dexter sat on the bed and reached out to touch Antonio's head. "A feedbag dinner is better than no dinner," said Dexter.

"I'm fucked up the ass, Dexter. I can't eat, can't go to the gym, haven't been to a party in four months. I'm not going to wait until I'm yellow skin stretched over bones.

"Don't worry," Antonio said again. "I have another friend."

***

Antonio looked dreadful, was dreadful to look at. It made Dexter sad to touch him. To see a human being writhing like a dying animal was something anyone would wish to avoid.

He couldn't remember the boy's name, or his face, but Dexter remembered how he and Antonio barricaded themselves in the bathroom at Joe's party, behind the hollow core door with the flimsy knob and twist lock. Dexter should have kicked it in and seen them holding each other, having met a mere thirty minutes earlier, tongues deep in each other's mouth, hands on each other's buttocks, cocks pressed against each other's groin. But he had remained outside, pounding on the door, screaming for Antonio to open up. Why didn't they have the decency to go somewhere else to escape detection? Initially Dexter couldn't even look at him, but after a flickering hesitation, after he had already considered the pleased expressions on the faces of the on-lookers, he had.

"I was drunk, Dexter. You know I love you."

***

"When did you start driving so aggressively?" said Antonio. Dexter had weaved in and out of the three lanes of Lake Shore Drive traffic as he always did, because he didn't really like driving anymore. He pulled into the hos-pital parking lot and told the attendant that he had an admission. A lie that would allow them to park at the yel-low curb, close to the entrance.

Dexter turned off the engine, got out, and went around the back of the car. He opened Antonio's door, but he made no immediate move. He stared, as usual, into the distance. Except for the remark about Dexter's driving, he'd been un-usually quiet. They inched up the walk and into the lobby and waited for the loaded gurney to come off the elevator: a white-haired patient from the geriatric floor.

Antonio stumbled onto the elevator, stubbing his toe at the threshold and grimaced.

"Are you in pain?" said Dexter.

"It's the neuropathy, Dexter. My body always hurts."

HIV patients were on four. One of the six people at the reception counter, a freckled girl with a Scottish accent, finally looked up and smiled. She directed them to the out-patient area of the floor; she'd page Sam and send him over.

They passed the rooms of people with mouths too shrunken to accommodate their teeth and sat down in a row of chairs in the hallway. A familiar gay porno star walked past with a boy dressed in white, a nurse or technician, who asked the celebrity if he had eaten. The handsome but miniaturized actor smiled and seemed to address his reply to Antonio: "I stopped for a cheeseburger and some fries." When the boy had disappeared around the corner, Antonio spoke: "And a couple of balls," he said, apparently intending his sarcasm for no one other than himself.

Sam appeared from around the same corner a moment later. He motioned for Antonio, and Dexter followed the two into an unoccupied room. After they hugged, Sam introduced himself to Dexter, and helped Antonio up onto the bed. Without instruction Antonio unbuttoned his flannel shirt and removed it. A nurse entered, put a thermometer in his mouth, and began to take his blood pressure. Sam wore a white shirt and tie and slacks; a stethoscope—an accessory in chrome and black rubber—hung round his neck. Sam, Antonio had said, was a Physician's Assistant and far more competent and caring than most of the doctors. Dexter sat on the green, vinyl couch and watched. Sam started to compile a list of the drugs Antonio was taking, but he put down the clipboard when Antonio said that he had stopped everything but Atavan, Tylenol, and Vicodin. After the nurse left, Sam examined Antonio's left arm, where the pic-line had been. "You should continue the Bactrim," he said. He warmed the metal flat part of the stethoscope by rubbing it in his palms and raised Antonio's tee shirt and began to listen as he automatically inhaled and exhaled. "Your lungs are clear; let's make sure they stay that way."

Antonio waited till Sam pulled his tee shirt down then he lay back on the bed. And stared into his eyes. "Are you going to give me the morphine?" he said.

Sam took Antonio's left arm and studied the surface just below the crook by running his fingers over the skin. "We'll have to put in a new line since you ripped the other one out."

"It was infected," said Antonio.

"You're sure about the morphine?"

"And what we talked about."

Sam let go of his arm and turned to Dexter. "Could you leave us alone for a few minutes?"

Up the hall a woman came out of a room on the right, carrying a Styrofoam cup, dividing her attention between it and the floor. Dexter went into the room she had emerged from, poured himself some overcooked coffee, and opened the refrigerator. Plastic containers of Jello and tuna salad and egg salad lined the shelves; he removed an assortment—six in all—and placed them on the counter to remove their lids. He found crackers and plastic forks and paper napkins in the overhead cabinets and, after ripping the cellophane off the crackers, began to eat, greedily, practically without chewing. He swallowed the coffee, wiped his mouth with a napkin, and returned to the area outside Antonio's temporary room in time to see the door open, and Sam, who told him to come back in.

Dexter approached the bed and watched the nurse probe Antonio's arm with a needle, attached to a short length of plastic tubing. "Is this the new picline?" said Dexter.

"It's a Streamline," said Antonio, grimacing again as the nurse searched for a vein. The door opened. Dexter looked at Sam who motioned for him to come back outside.

"He can't be alone on morphine. Are you going to be able to stay with him?"

"I'm not sure," said Dexter.

"Has he told you what's happening?"

And then Sam explained that Antonio had decided on the following Wednesday as the day. He explained about the morphine and said he would call Dexter to give him details outside the hospital. "He wants to stay with you till then. We'll need you to sign some papers. A power-of-attorney will protect you from Natalie."

***

Antonio was not an intellectual, but he had the wisdom to seek out the emotionally dependent. He didn't care if others paid the mortgage and bought the groceries. When he felt bad he got a haircut and bought a pair of shoes that he didn't need. He put on a pair of tight pants and a tank top and went to the bar, and by the time he got off work he had arranged to go home with someone.

Now, after all these years, he wanted to die in Dexter's house. A week before Christmas. Dexter didn't even think he believed in suicide, though he couldn't pretend to comprehend his friend's pain. And then there was Natalie.

Sam called it simple. Antonio would go to sleep. Sam spelled out the technicalities: an injection to prevent vomiting; a bolus of morphine; a cocktail of vodka, cranberry juice, and the contents of thirty Seconals.

Antonio would go to sleep. What did death mean to him? Nothingness?

And to Dexter?

Leaves drop from trees, fertilize the soil. Energy is transformed. But what about memory?

And what about suffering? Should we embrace the pain to move beyond it? Would suffering prepare us for a later existence without pain?

And Antonio would go to sleep.

***

Dexter hadn't expected Natalie. Still, he instructed the doorman to send her up. He hesitated before greeting her at his door, and he hesitated a few seconds longer before standing back and asking her inside. "I've been meaning to call," he said.

He hadn't because of the plan. Yes, people deserved the truth. But the truth would undo Natalie.

"He belongs with me and the boys. We're his family." Natalie's eyes teared.

"Maybe he came here to protect you?" said Dexter.

"From what?"

"He's not taking his medicine," said Dexter.

He had given up. Dexter had tried repeatedly to elicit some sign of a wish to live. He'd read to Antonio: fiction, poetry, newspapers, magazines, inspirational texts about life and death; he'd played music on the stereo: Baroque concertos, Romantic symphonies, jazz, pop, rhythm and blues; he'd rented movies: Hollywood classics, French comedies, English melodramas. Once, during a recording of the Dvorak Cello Concerto, Dexter thought he had succeeded. He related how the young soloist had been struck down by a paralyzing disease in mid-career, but had continued to teach others even after her fingers had become too crippled to demonstrate bowing technique, and during the final movement, as the cello sang with the passion of a human voice, Antonio sat up, leaned back against the arm of the sofa, closed his eyes, and moved his head and shoulders ever so slightly with the music. Even so subtle a reaction brought tears to Dexter's eyes, but none so far as he could tell, to his friend's.

"I'll talk to him," said Natalie.

Dexter led her to the living room and Natalie took a seat on the sofa, facing the lake. She peered out through the wall of glass for a while and blinked. CEO had wandered into the room and was rubbing back and forth against Natalie's legs. She looked down and started when the cat leaped up abruptly onto her lap. Then Natalie's lips parted, signaling that she was ready to talk. Dexter expected a comment first about the cat or the view or the weather when she began to speak in a slow, measured cadence.

"When we were children, I was the one who saw to it that he cleaned his room and helped Mother clear the table. She always spoiled him. He got more presents for his birthday—and at Christmas. He had his own car in high-school. He didn't have to be home early. He could date who he wanted." Natalie took a breath as if to gain the courage to reveal what disturbed her the most. Her voice quivered. "Though of course Mother didn't know that, even in school, he had a reputation."

Natalie looked at Dexter, and he was about to suggest that she go into the bedroom to see Antonio, when he appeared. Dexter saw him first because he faced the back of the room. Antonio smiled and came around the sofa, staggering at the edge. He carried the morphine pump like a purse. Dexter stood and quickly took hold of him round the waist and helped navigate around the glass coffee table to a place on the sofa next to Natalie. Natalie's mouth opened, but she didn't actually gasp.

"You've lost more weight, honey," she said. She looked at the pump but didn't ask about it. "You need the TPN." She stroked his hair, smoothed it behind his ear.

Antonio looked at Dexter. "Now where is it we're going?" he said. "The symphony?" Natalie frowned.

"We're staying home," said Dexter. "Remember, we're going to rent a movie." And then to Natalie, "It's the morphine. He gets confused."

"Don't you want to come home for Christmas?" said Natalie. "Don't you want to be home with me and the boys?" Antonio smiled and looked vacantly into the room—at no one or nothing in particular it seemed. "Dexter can spend Christmas Eve with us," she said.

***

From his position in the kitchen, as he scoured the sink and shined the faucet, Dexter could see through the dining room window to the lights of Wrigley Field; when the blinds were canted in the right direction, as they were now, he could see, through this same window, the empty docks of Belmont Harbor. The mirror on the dining room wall revealed the back of Antonio's head and shoulders, on the living room sofa, attached by tubing to the cad pump of morphine. Dexter put down the sponge, rinsed away the cleansing powder, and walked into the room. Perhaps Sam had already left the parking garage and was approaching the lobby.

Dexter went to the dining room window and cracked it open. The wind blew steady and cold off the water. In the park below he saw a solitary couple walking toward the shore, pushed along by the current of air; dressed in hooded parkas, they huddled close and held hands. Dexter scanned the row of parked cars on Diversey Avenue, as if he might actually be able to catch a glimpse of Sam. It was already six-thirty; Sam had said he would arrive by six.

Antonio had been on the phone most of the afternoon, talking to friends; a few had stopped by: most of them Dexter didn't recognize. But one, a bartender from a club on Clark Street, took Dexter aside and asked: "Is something up?" Dexter felt it was Antonio's right to reveal his plans. But then said: "He's tired of it all."

While he stood with the boy in the hallway, Sam stepped out of the elevator down the hall. He saw Dexter and walked toward him, carrying a valise and a shopping bag. He hugged Dexter and looked at the boy, but Dexter did not introduce them to each other; Dexter shook the boy's hand, thanked him for coming, and led Sam inside, leaving the boy outside.

Sam put down his valise and took the shopping bag over and set it down on the sofa. He put his hand on the back of Antonio's neck, leaned over, and kissed him on the cheek. Sam talked in hushed tones, but Antonio merely nodded in assent or shook his head. After a few minutes, Dexter heard Sam say: "I'll wait in the bedroom; take your time."

He got up, retrieved his valise, asked Dexter to show him the bedroom, and once there, opened his case and took out several items: a stethoscope, a Mason jar of liquid, several syringes, alcohol swipes, and medicines. He handed the jar of liquid to Dexter. "Put this in the fridge for me, would you?" he said. "Do you have any vodka?" Dexter nodded. "Could I have a vodka cranberry, or vodka orange?" Dexter nodded again. "You might want to make one for yourself too," he said, as Dexter walked to the door.

From the kitchen, he saw that Antonio held the phone to his ear, but he was not talking. Dexter mixed the drinks, took a large swallow and went into the room and sat next to Antonio. "Are you on hold?" said Dexter.

"They hung up," said Antonio. He set the phone on the table, put his hand in his lap, and stared out at the lake. Dexter reached over, wrapped his hand around Antonio's cold, smooth fingers.

"What's in the bag?" said Dexter.

Antonio looked at it. "Oh, your present. Don't open it till Christmas."

"I love you," said Dexter. "Are you sure you wouldn't rather wait?"

Antonio didn't reply, and when Sam came up behind the sofa, and touched him on the back of the neck, he stood. Sam took hold of his shoulders and led him down the hall. Dexter took another swallow of his drink and looked at the shopping bag. He removed the wrapped package, shook it gently, tried to estimate its weight. It seemed the perfect occasion to cry, but he felt nothing—or numb at best—and crying would be like draining the liquid from a blister. Temporary relief. It would take a long time for the tender skin to toughen.

Sam called to Dexter from down the hall, and he put the package back in the bag and got up.

Antonio lay in bed, propped up by pillows. He smiled at Dexter. And then he closed his eyes.

On a late summer afternoon, a year or so after Peru, after Dexter had gone to see Machu Picchu alone because Antonio hadn't made it back to the room in time for the train, and long after Antonio realized that Dexter was serious about ending their friendship, they'd run into one another outside Water Tower Place on Michigan Avenue. Antonio had already moved away; Dexter heard from someone that he was living in Atlanta, from someone else that he was in New Orleans, and from still another, who had seen him on Fire Island, that he was tending bar in Florida.

Dexter had been looking at a display in the Marshall Field's window and hadn't seen Antonio approach.

He had appeared without warning next to Dexter, dressed in a faded red tee shirt, torn cutoff jeans, and sandals. His smooth arms and legs were burnt sienna brown and his face, framed in black curls, was illuminated by the red rays of the evening sun. He'd been in town for a week, he said, and just spent the day at Oak Street Beach. He smiled, removed his sunglasses, blinked through heavy lashes, and shook his head as if puzzled. Then he put his arms around Dexter and kissed him lightly on the mouth. "You're the classiest man around," he said. And he had turned and walked away.

Antonio's brow was wrinkled now, and his cheeks sunken. His breathing had slowed. And ceased intermittently in apneic moments till his body abruptly shook, expelling carbon dioxide in a wet gurgling echo through his open mouth. He still wore the baseball cap; it rested crookedly, larger than ever, on his wizened head. Antonio was dissolving inside his pullover and sweatpants. Dexter sat at the bottom of the bed, held on to Antonio's ankle, buried his face in the crook of his free arm, and cried. Sam held his stethoscope against Antonio's chest and waited. The intervals between the hollow exhalations lengthened until, after about twenty minutes, Antonio's body lay still and unmoving and Sam said: "He's gone."

Later that night when Dexter was drunk and Sam had gone away too, after Dexter had watched as the two heavy men wearing white shirts and black ties zipped Antonio's body up in the bag and hauled him to the freight elevator, Dexter sat at his dining table gripping his glass of melting ice. The white package, tied up in red ribbon, sat on the table in front of him. He listened to the roar of the wind off the lake. The wall of glass was all that separated Dexter from the ever-growing storm outside. It whistled over the gaps around the waist-high casement windows at the bottom and slammed at the ceiling-high immovable glass panes that enclosed the dining and living rooms. Cars moved in steady ribbons on both sides of Lake Shore. The night before he had stayed in bed with Antonio's arm across his waist and his friend's head nestled on his chest. They had always slept well together: that had been the best part. But last night, Dexter lay awake listening to the beating of his own heart and the sound of Antonio's irregular breathing.

In Natalie's Heaven, he supposed, friends and family sat together on the edge of fleecy clouds, under God's watchful eye, looking through old photo albums. For his part, Dexter doubted that physicality even applied. Perhaps, though, there was one collective, conscious soul existing in a state of euphoric bliss.

Dexter stood, walked into the living room, and looked east over the lake. The moon, low and not yet full, shone on the water's surface, illuminating the waves and the beach. Below, a lone man, dressed in dark clothes and carrying a knapsack, struggled into the gale, across the park. He arrived at a trash barrel, in front of the entrance to the closed miniature golf course. Without relinquishing his hold on his satchel, he stooped over the barrel and began methodically to pick through the rubbish.

Antonio had gone to sleep. Dexter reached down and unclamped the casement window to let in the cold air. He moved to the next window, and the next, and the next, until every window in the room was open. Then he dropped to his knees and closed his eyes. The brittle air smelled faintly of smoke.

Necessary Repairs

Work on the building's exterior began in June, after the cold rains of May had ended. Pneumatic hammers and chisels beat out a relentless tattoo, signalling the arrival of summer heat and humidity; the vibration of hardened steel on concrete echoed throughout the interior of all forty-three floors. The letter from the condominium association said the work would continue through August.

Once Dexter Giles had wished to live to be a hundred. Travel he insisted would sustain him. Following world news and developments would be enough he said to make him rise early each day and make his pot of coffee. Reading the newspaper first thing, seated in the chair by the window that overlooked the lake, had been a considerable pleasure for years now, and something he had thought he would always treasure. Buying flowers, he maintained, would continue to bring brightness to his house and his spirits. Painting a room, buying a new table or appliance, following the ups and downs of his investments would always energize him, he had believed. A trip to the grocery where he bantered with his favorite cashier, a seat on the sidewalk terrace for an afternoon coffee, a trip to the dry cleaners, an occasional matinee to escape amongst the mist-covered hills of an English romance: this would suffice, given the promise of continued good health, to provide the will to live.

So Dexter Giles had thought. But not now. Time no longer had dimension. It passed with such rapidity that it became impossible to measure, and yet he dragged through each day wishing only for the sun to set on his boredom. He retired earlier and earlier each night and awoke long before sunrise as a consequence.

Dexter replenished CEO's supply of fresh water, filled his dish with fresh food, and left the kitchen. Taking his wallet and keys from the table in the entrance foyer, he stepped into the hallway and locked the door to his apartment. In the elevator he tried to formulate a plan for the day. He dismissed the idea of a visit to the Art Institute: he had no desire to make the trip into the city in a bus choked with people. In the lobby he nodded at Al, who uttered some inanity about the White Sox, and hastened to the revolving doors before he could be drawn into a conversation.

Without conscious decision he turned left and walked toward the lake. He would sit on the rocks at the water's edge and watch the boats. He took pleasure in the spectacle of such a large body of fresh water, which in many ways was like gazing out over an ocean, whose distant shore could not be seen. But of course, though he couldn't see the shore, he knew that it was simply Michigan over there. And he'd been to Michigan and had no desire to go back.

At the edge of Lincoln Park, not even halfway to the lakefront, Dexter turned and headed in the opposite direction, back through his neighborhood with its mixture of older people who had money and too much time and the younger who overflowed with optimism at the start of their careers. The veterans occupied the towers that lined the park and Lake Shore Drive; the ingenues lived inland, in the buildings with six to twelve units. He passed the flower shop and the coffee bar and entered the supermarket with the excuse of buying dental floss.

Dexter took a hand-carried basket and walked down the aisle marked *Toiletries*. A precocious couple stood in front of the shampoos and conditioners, withdrawing bottles to read the labels and study the ingredients, before replacing them to take up others. They stood close to each other, touching at the shoulder, and occasionally the girl used her free hand to rub her friend's back. Dexter imagined them in a Chinese restaurant interrogating the waiter: "No MSG. Right?"

At the end of the aisle he located the toothpaste and dental floss. The couple examining the shampoos would probably descend into madness at the prospect of choosing between *waxed* or *unwaxed* and *mint* or *unflavored*. Dexter dropped the least expensive brand in his basket.

He was about to roam the store for impulse purchases when he heard: "Dexter? Dexter Giles?"

He turned. For a moment he couldn't place the face. She had changed her hair color to blond—inappropriate considering her age—and the flesh under her neck and chin sagged perilously. "Tula," said Dexter, as if to himself, and then before he could stop he smiled and stuck out his hand. "I thought you lived in Mt. Prospect or someplace. What brings you to the city?"

"You're looking very fit and healthy," said Tula. "Do you jog or something?"

"I owe it all to kick-boxing." Dexter patted his stomach. "It's one hell of a workout." Tula's face registered a look of astonishment. "Yesterday at the gym," said Dexter, "I gave a woman such a thrashing. My arms and calves were so pumped with blood that they literally throbbed. And she was bigger than me and at least ten years older."

"Still the smart ass, I see. Well whatever it is, it's working."

"Weights for a while. But then I quit. Now I just walk a lot to get out of the apartment."

"I cook when I get depressed," said Tula. "Do you miss Impco?"

"The travel would finish me off these days," said Dexter. "Is your mother still—"

"She's ninety-two and listens to every Cub game on the radio," said Tula. "She's practically blind and doesn't get around very well, but she goes on. What a lost cause." A woman couldn't get her cart past Tula and Dexter, standing as they were rather far apart and blocking the aisle, so Tula moved out of the way and looked at the woman with annoyance.

"The Cubs are a lost cause," said Dexter. Tula looked at him again and screwed her face.

"I meant—" said Tula.

"I know," said Dexter.

She looked up the aisle and then down at her hand-held basket. "I suppose I should get my things—I came in to kill some time—and go. I'm meeting my niece for coffee."

And then Dexter said it was awfully nice seeing her and she said likewise and when she had walked a few feet away, Dexter said, "Do you come into town often to see your niece?"

"She not really my niece. She grew up next door and we've stayed in touch. But yes, lately I've been coming every other week."

"Maybe we'll run into each other again."

"That would be nice," said Tula.

***

The chiselling, grinding, grating vibration of the workmen's tools reverberated in the roots of his teeth. Dexter slammed his book down on the arm of his chair and turned on the television. The DOW was up. The NASDAQ down. He scanned the channels. A man with long bleached hair was crying as he described the power of Jesus's love. A woman's hand twisted from side to side to catch the light on her bejeweled finger as she cautioned the buyers to act fast before the supply of exquisite rings was exhausted. The noise insinuated itself into every fiber of his body and exhausted him. June was barely two weeks over; he felt as if he were standing in the middle of a subway construction site. If only he had the energy to go somewhere for the summer. He flipped the channel again. The Cubs were behind eight to two.

He'd been to the supermarket several times in the last two weeks, but he hadn't run into Tula. Recently he'd had little contact with people. The noise had put him into such a deep depression that he could barely manage trivial conversation. He hadn't phoned Delia for weeks now. If he made the effort she would no doubt cheer him: she was a storyteller and there would be plenty of tales about how Mark's wife wasn't breast feeding the baby and how Taylor had dumped his latest girlfriend. Then Delia would ask him to come for a visit—a visit that he had no desire to make. For all the complaints she had had about their mother, she had continued to grow more and more like her as she aged.

When the telephone rang, Dexter assumed he would have to say once again that he didn't wish to change his long distance service. "I got your number from information," said Tula. "I hope it's all right. I'm coming in to see my niece and I thought you might want to have coffee." Dexter looked through the door into the kitchen, at the clock above the second door which led to the hallway. The grinding noise grew louder, more insistent.

Dexter raised his voice. "What time? And where?" he said.

***

They chose a table on the sidewalk. "I thought I wouldn't miss Mother; that I'd like living alone," said Tula. "But I was already past fifty when I finally got the chance to find out."

"Are you still in touch with Jim Gallagher?" said Dexter.

"I get a Christmas card every year, with a note."

"That's it?"

"His wife has brain cancer. They gave her a year."

"I heard that Ernie Gastineau died of cancer, a year ago. What's with all the cancer?" said Dexter.

"He'll have to learn to go it alone, just like we all do eventually," said Tula.

"Classical music used to do it for me. Or reading. And there was a time when I could go alone to see a movie, but now—"

"He had no guilt about leaving me alone when he retired to Florida. Men are selfish bastards," said Tula.

"Yes, aren't they?" said Dexter.

Tula threw back her head and laughed.

"What about your friend who used to call? What happened to him?" said Tula.

"Jean Paul. He lived with me a few times over the years. We were merely friends. I was a safe haven. He bounced from job to job with grandiose plans, never quite understanding that hard work would win out over connections and lucky breaks. He cost me plenty but I enjoyed his humor—and I felt sorry for him. In the end he did fine. He lives in Tangier, but phones occasionally.

"Do you think you'll hear from Gallagher, after his wife—" and here Dexter paused. Perhaps he had presumed too much, though a tone of familiarity had developed between them that made it seem appropriate.

"I don't think I'm that special. So he'd take me to lunch, see me once or twice a week and give me the line that he couldn't get a divorce until his kids grew up, and after they went off to college there was another reason. He occupied just enough space to prevent me from being open to meeting someone I could have had a real relationship with. Not just this fantasy. If he walked in here right now, I'd spit in his face," said Tula.

"Office romances seldom work."

Tula stared at Dexter. "You look good. Really good. Are you happy?"

"I'm a little bored."

***

Early in the week, he telephoned Delia. He would have mentioned his depression but she would probably have told him to join a group or answer an ad. He made a call to Jean Paul in Tangier too. He sounded a little lonely; he didn't mention any new young boys.

Tula didn't call so he didn't meet her for coffee.

On Tuesday of the following week, after enduring the workmen's assault on the building all morning, he had gone to a movie. He had tried, unsuccessfully, to tell himself that

the purpose of the deafening racket was to make the struc-
ture safer and sturdier, but on Monday he had gone outside
to check the progress and discovered, when he looked up at
the platform being used by the workmen, that the crew con-
sisted of but two scruffy men. Two men. To grind,
pulverize, and eat at the entire surface of a forty-storey
building. Why, it was madness. No wonder the work was
going to take all summer. He had stormed back into his unit
and checked the movie schedule and left immediately. At
the theater he had the idea of inviting Tula to go with him
to another movie the next day, even though he thought her
taste might make it difficult to agree on what to see.

The double ring of the telephone announced her arrival
in the lobby. He turned on the coffee pot, glanced at the
vase of tulips on the table in the dining area, and looked at
himself in the hallway mirror.

At the sound of the brass knocker he opened the door.
Tula wore a yellow dress and matching high-heeled shoes,
as if prepared to attend an Easter church service. Dexter
must have looked surprised. "I get so few chances to dress
up and I thought you might want to have some dinner later."
And then on entering the living room she said: "What a
wonderful view. I'd never get tired of a view like this." She
took a seat on the sectional sofa facing the lake to the east.
"What's that noise?" she said, glancing around the room as
if to find the source.

"They're removing chipped concrete on the outside,"
said Dexter. "Coffee?" He went to the kitchen and poured
two cups and returned to the living room. "Our movie
starts at two. I hope you like history. We're seeing a movie
about Queen Victoria." He sat across from her in the swivel
chair.

"Should I have worn a hat?"

"That's amusing," said Dexter.

Dexter's cat jumped up onto Tula's lap. "Aren't you the
friendly one," she said. "But you're the wrong shade of
yellow.

Dexter started to get up to retrieve the animal, but Tula had already lifted him up and set him on the floor. "That's CEO," said Dexter, "though he likes people too much to ever really be a CEO."

"I'm surprised they allow pets in your building."

"Actually, they don't"

"My god, that noise is irritating," said Tula. "Does it go on all day?"

"From 8:30 to 5:30," said Dexter.

"It's like being in the dentist's chair without novocaine," said Tula.

Dexter smiled.

They relaxed too long over coffee and had to rush to make the two o'clock starting time. One advantage to going alone was not feeling responsible for someone else. Dexter remembered that Tula's comments could rankle too, though they had reconciled long ago. Still, he was concerned that she would approve of his choice. He was concerned too that she was a talker. He couldn't stand people who chattered and commented before the film's conclusion.

At first, during the previews and for ten minutes or so into the film, he watched her, but she seemed interested, perhaps more so because she didn't care whether he liked or disliked the movie. She didn't talk at all, though she smacked her lips occasionally as she tore off a piece of red licorice candy with her protruding front teeth.

On the way out of the theater, he waited for her reaction. "Well?" he said at last.

"I guess the moral of the story is that even a queen needs a man to make her happy," said Tula. "Are you hungry?"

At the restaurant they took a table by the window. Dexter wanted to discuss the film, but after they had settled and ordered, Tula said she'd heard from a friend at Imperial that Jim Gallagher's wife was not responding to therapy. She said she heard the woman had lost her short-term memory, though she spoke often and with clarity about childhood friends. "I suppose when she does go they'll have a service here. Both of their girls live in Olympia Fields."

"Would you attend?" said Dexter.

"I don't know. You could come with me. He'd love to see you." Tula grunted a laugh. It was meant to be laughter anyway, but her recollection of the incident seemed to prevent real mirth.

And why not? Dexter would be the first to admit that it no doubt had been a difficult time for her. But he wouldn't take the blame for her lover's misdeeds. "He got himself fired; I just exposed him," said Dexter. "Would you like some wine?"

After ordering the wine and dinner Dexter brought up a number of subjects in an attempt to find common ground. Besides work, he found, there were few. She discussed her niece in a way that revealed herself as a meddler. Tula also sewed, knitted, and painted miniature, ceramic objects. At present she was working on several Christmas trees that lit up when plugged into an electrical outlet. She made a face when she tasted her radicchio and said she planned to distribute the miniature trees to neighbors and friends during the holidays. Dexter wondered if she had many friends and who they were.

During the main course he mentioned the symphony. He watched as she raked the truffle bits off her chicken breast and pushed them to the side. Tula said she had been to the *Nutcracker* once, years ago. Then he mentioned the Booker Prize novel he had recently finished. Tula made another face as she chewed on a leek. She didn't have much time for books, she said, but she had read a biography on Frank Sinatra by Kitty Kelley. She had never travelled much either, not even after her mother went to the nursing home. Jim Gallagher had taken her to Las Vegas for a long weekend, but that was before it had become the attraction of today. Eventually, by default, they got back to the subject of the people they'd both known at Imperial. They laughed together about Gastineau, the man they had worked for after Tula's transfer, the way his white, hairless ankles were revealed when he tried to cross his plump legs, and his penchant for producing pointless, procedural memoranda. Nevertheless, by the time dessert came they were both suppressing yawns. And yet when Tula said, "It's my turn to pick next time," Dexter found himself enthusiastic, though he wondered if he could endure a Kevin Costner film.

***

Dexter awoke at 6:00 A.M. and made his bed. He prepared a pot of coffee, fed CEO, and wiped the countertops, though they glistened already. He retrieved the paper from the hallway, went into his den, and turned on the television to review the market's progress, which at the moment was coming back slightly from a 200-point drop. "The fundamentals are sound," said the analyst, and Dexter snorted. He walked to the living room. Not a cushion was out of place; not even a crumb or a thread littered the carpet. He prepared a breakfast of egg whites and dry toast, sat in the dining nook, and ate slowly. After finishing, he rinsed his plate and utensils and put them in the dishwasher rack. There was no need to start the appliance because as yet he hadn't accumulated enough dirty dishes. The forecast was for continued hot and humid weather, and he had no inspiration as how to spend the day. At eight o'clock he returned to the den and sat in the wingback chair and opened his book. The suddenness of the grinding and hammering at 8:20 A.M. startled him. How long before his chair began to vibrate and jiggle across the floor? Today was different. When the tools attacked the concrete surface, the clamor was jingling, almost musical, but when the air jack slipped and made contact with the metal of the window frames, the racket had the urgency of a rapid-fire assault weapon.

He called Tula to suggest lunch—and a trip to the Lincoln Park Conservatory to see the summer show of tropical plants—instead of a movie. "Le Restaurant would be perfect," said Dexter. "It's directly across the street facing the park." What she might wear hadn't occurred to him, but in his most fantastic imagination he couldn't have concocted the ensemble she sported when he met her on the sidewalk outside the restaurant a little past noon. He had no idea one could still purchase stone-washed jeans and the waist-length, sequined, purple denim top reminded him of those jackets the bullfighters wore.

"That's quite a jacket," said Dexter.

"I made it myself," said Tula.

He leaned in close, removed his glasses, and focused on a particularly large rhinestone which served as a rooster's eye. "It must have taken you hours," he said.

The waiter didn't pay any attention to her clothing when he offered the menus, but Dexter saw the busboy cast a sidelong glance at the coat when he emerged from behind to pour ice water into her glass. Dexter hadn't seen the back of the coat. Was there a depiction of two roosters entangled in battle?

"Next time I should invite my niece. You'd like her," said Tula. She opened her menu. "What do you recommend?"

"The workmen started before eight-thirty this morning." He rubbed both temples with his hands. "My head is humming like a tuning fork. I swear if I close my eyes, I can still hear the morons," said Dexter. He studied the menu and took a sip of water.

"I have aspirin," said Tula.

"Hmm. This is new. *Curls of Eggplant and Sole.* And this too. *Smoked Salmon Parcels with Sea Bass Mousse.* Would you care for some wine? Should I get a bottle?"

After they ordered and were eating, Tula looked up from her *Rolled Breast of Chicken Parmesan.* "Remember when we had coffee that first day after we ran into each other at the market?" said Tula. Dexter took a sip of wine and nodded. "I asked you about your friend that used to call at the office." He nodded again. "I meant the young one. What ever happened to him?"

"Antonio," said Dexter. He put down his wine glass and wiped his mouth with his napkin. "He died."

"I'm sorry," said Tula. "Was it—?"

"He died in my apartment, actually. Almost three years ago now. Yes, it was."

"He was always so friendly on the phone. He seemed real nice."

"He could be quite charming."

"Were you two—were you friends for a long time?"

"He lived with me for a year. I never heard much from him until he got sick years later. Then he sort of showed up on my doorstep one day looking like a cadaver. His only family was a sister—a religious fanatic—and he wanted to get away from her."

"Only a year?" said Tula.

"On the plus side, Antonio was often a good companion. He made me laugh, he was great to look at, and I think underneath it all he had a good heart. But, and it's a big but, he had a drug problem, he lied and cheated, he was the absolute master of bullshit, and I finally had enough and ended our relationship during a trip to Peru."

"At least you had the sense to say *enough*. I never did understand what Jim was like until he was gone."

"Well you knew he was going home to his wife at night. I could never have stood for that."

"You'd be surprised what you might do when someone says they love you. I waited many Friday nights when he never showed and didn't call. All day Saturday and Sunday I'd wait to hear from him to explain and I'd be so pissed off that I couldn't wait to get to work on Monday to let him have it."

"That was your problem. Letting him have it," said Dexter.

Tula lowered her voice and adopted a southern accent. "'I'm sorry, Tu. Louise planned a damned cocktail party for the neighbors and I forgot all about it. I tried all weekend to get to the phone, but she was all over me like a cheap suit.'

"First thing I did when she called was say 'How was your cocktail party, Mrs. Gallagher?' 'Honey,' she said, 'that was over a month ago.'

"And he complained about her all the time. She was too fat, she was a nag, she was no fun. He told me he hadn't had sex with her for two years because she didn't smell as pretty as I did. God, I wonder what he said about me.

"'I love you, Tu', he'd say. Then he would wink and say, 'Let's take a long lunch.' That's all it took and I'd forget about being mad."

Dexter understood. A person susceptible to flattery is an easy mark. "He stole from the company and cheated on his wife and children. You shouldn't have thought you'd be treated differently."

Now Tula took a sip of wine.

They finished eating and asked for the check. Tula agreed to split it without an individual accounting. Dexter had half expected her to behave the way the secretaries at Imperial had when the bill came. He had enjoyed listening to the hens quibble and attempt to account for every nickel. "I only had a salad and a glass of wine," was a popular disclaimer.

Inside the Conservatory they walked among the palms and ferns. The humid air was sweet and musky. Water dripped from overhanging fronds and leaves onto their clothing. Dexter had come here alone many times. It was soothing and peaceful. Like walking inside a giant terrarium. At the restaurant Tula had gotten quiet, and Dexter thought she might be brooding. But then at the Conservatory she regained her initial disposition and made almost constant *ooh* and *aah* noises, and Dexter began to wish that he were alone.

"Did you ever have a thing for a woman?" said Tula, glancing quickly at him.

"I'm afraid not," said Dexter.

***

Dexter sat in the wingback chair with his book. The grinding of the workmen's tools vibrated around him, from every direction. The ceiling, the floor, the walls. It was Monday; the racket had intensified after the weekend interruption. Were they moving closer to his floor? He turned the page of his book, then turned another without absorbing the text. At last he put down the book and walked into the hallway. From here he could see CEO lying asleep on the ottoman against the window. Somewhere he had read that dogs slept fourteen hours a day and he thought it strange that he didn't know the corresponding fact about cats, though he'd had cats since he was a child. If only he could sleep fourteen hours a day. Perhaps then the days would be easier to endure. There was that joke about cats thinking about food, sex, and nothing and after they were neutered they thought about food and nothing. Dexter might as well be a cat. Food and nothing.

***

Spending the Fourth of July at Arlington Park was Tula's idea. They met at the edge of the VIP parking lot, at the entrance to the clubhouse level. Tula was dressed rather well, by her standards, wearing a dark-print cotton dress and a straw hat. Her sunglasses, though, were oversized and matronly.

In the grandstand she sat, smoothed her skirt, and opened her racing form. "Jim and I used to come to the old track, before it burned down," she said. "God, that man could pick the horses."

"How did you manage?"

"What?"

"To be here at the same time?"

"Are you auditing me, Dexter?" said Tula.

"I'm curious about the logistics. That's all."

"Jim would leave the office for a meeting and I'd schedule some personal business. We'd drive out separately, like you and I did."

"Weren't you worried about getting caught?"

"Jim was, but I was younger. I wanted people to know."

The need to hide a private life was something he and Gallagher had had in common. Though to be sure the consequences of discovery had different implications for the two of them. Having a mistress was required behavior for management at Imperial. Having a male lover was grounds for dismissal.

Dexter bet cautiously, wagering no more than five dollars on a given race, but Tula was more aggressive, and after the finish of the fifth race she was ahead by a hundred dollars. Dexter was ahead too, but by a margin of less than thirty. An announcement over the public address system indicated that Bountiful had been scratched from the sixth race. "Harass has been scratched," said Dexter, recalling the old radio blooper. "Scratch Harass."

Tula laughed. "Have another beer," she said. "You're funny when you're drunk.

Dexter did indeed feel a bit tipsy and decided to bet a bit more aggressively on the remaining races. Tula liked a filly named Glacier in the eighth race. The odds were ten-to-one, but the horse had run well in her last two outings. "Let's go down to the paddock and check her out," said Tula.

Glacier was a beautiful, flea-bitten gray. She pranced and snorted and looked very much like a winner. "We could be conservative and bet her to place or show," said Dexter, looking at his tip sheet again.

"No way. This girl's going to win," said Tula.

They rushed to the betting windows and returned to their seats. Tula had wagered a hundred dollars and Dexter had bet fifty. On the back stretch Glacier brought up the rear and neither Dexter nor his rowdy friend had much to cheer about. But when in the far turn the filly made her move and began to catch up, both of them began to jump and yell. By the time the horses crossed the finish line Tula, hoarse herself now, grabbed Dexter's arm and closed her eyes. It wasn't until the results of the photo finish were announced, and they learned that Glacier had come second by a nare, that Dexter revealed that he had bet the steed to place.

"You're a sneaky bastard," said Tula.

***

Tula didn't telephone every day but she rarely went more than three days without getting in touch with him to talk about her mother and her niece. She seldom hung up before getting in a comment about her former lover either, a fact that irritated Dexter in a way he didn't fully comprehend. She was still smitten, indeed her long-time affair with the pompous executive seemed to have been the defining event in her life, and it irked him to see someone so addicted to mistreatment.

Dexter checked his watch, then went downstairs to the lobby for his morning mail. As he passed the door to the building office, he saw one of the two contractors coming out. The man wore a threadbare tee shirt with dark ochre stains around the armpits and he hadn't shaved, it appeared, for several days. He wore his dirty, brown hair in a pony tail, and a cigarette dangled from his lips. He smiled at Dexter and said, "Good day for a beer, eh?"

"Lovely," said Dexter.

***

Throughout the remainder of July and into August Dexter and Tula met at least once a week. As a rule, except for their trip to the Conservatory, he had waited for her invitations and followed her suggestions as to what to do or where to go. Gradually though, he grew tired of shopping excursions and always found her selections, at least in the clothing department, hideous.

Dexter rubbed his face with his palms and then clamped them over his ears. He could still hear the hum and clang of the equipment. A post-modern composition worthy of Hell. The unceasing, high-pitched whirr, like that of a bloated vacuum cleaner, punctuated by staccato percussive assaults on the concrete and metal was more even, on this day, than CEO could bear. The cat lay on the sunny, window ledge in an agitated state, eyes narrow, tail thumping, licking angrily at an upturned paw.

Dexter discarded the junk mail in the waste can, put the bills in a stack on his desk, and reached over and took up the phone. When Tula answered, he said: "If you're not busy, let's go for a drive."

"I should clean my house," she said.

"Let's go to Springfield. We can visit Lincoln's house and his tomb."

"How romantic," said Tula, and then after a pause, "Sure. Why not?"

When he picked her up and on the drive south Tula seemed preoccupied. Dexter complained about the workmen but she merely looked out the window at the boring landscape and said, suppressing a yawn, "It's still going on?" He attempted to discuss the book of essays he was reading and she nodded halfheartedly. He suggested they should go see the new film about Tibet next week, and she simply smoothed her dress and said nothing.

During the tour of Lincoln's home she barely glanced into the roped-off bedrooms and complained that her feet hurt when they left the house. At the cemetery she listened to Dexter's description of his year-ago visit to the Ford Theater, but he could see that she wasn't really listening. He suggested they stop for a sandwich and coffee before heading back to Chicago, and she looked at her watch before agreeing.

In the car, back on the interstate, Tula bit at her thumbnail.

"Is your mother all right?" said Dexter.

"She'll live to be a hundred," said Tula.

"And your niece. She's okay?"

"Oh yes."

Dexter kept his eyes on the highway ahead. Tula pulled down her sun visor, flipped up the mirror cover, and began to apply fresh lipstick. "And your health is good too," said Dexter.

Tula clamped the top on her lipstick, turned to face Dexter, and said, "Why?"

"You've barely said three words all day. I thought maybe the bank is repossessing your house, or your car blew up, or your mother is so despondent over the Cubs' lousy season that she killed herself, or you just discovered that your father was a guard at Auschwitz, or—"

"Shut up, Dexter. You should be happy, I'm not talking. Noise bothers you so much."

Twenty minutes passed—he knew because he kept checking the clock on the dash—before either of them uttered a sound. There was only the hum of the tires on the road and the wind rushing over the car, fleeting and transitory as life itself.

"Louise Gallagher died," said Tula. "Last night."

***

Wednesday Dexter awoke before sunrise to the sound of rain and thunder. He peered at the clock on the nightstand and squinted to make sure that he had read the dimly-lit numbers correctly. It was 4:30 A.M. and that meant that the forecast for showers had been correct, but early. For a while Dexter lingered in bed and listened. He tried to doze again, but was completely awake and so got out of bed. CEO eyed him from his chair by the window but made no move to get up. Dexter peered into Lincoln Park below. The rain fell so steadily that he could barely see the lights that lined the drive at the drive's perimeter. He brewed his coffee and started for the outside hallway to get the paper, but it was too early for the delivery.

He took his position in the wingback chair and opened his book and read without interruption until the sky gradually brightened and the rain stopped. By eight o'clock the sky had cleared completely, and Dexter realized that his hopes for one uninterrupted day of wet gloom had evaporated along with the precipitation. At eight-thirty the workmen resumed their assault on the building exterior with their tools. Dexter went to the stereo in the living room, searched through the collection of discs, and selected the Grieg Piano Concerto. He turned the volume high and lay back on the sofa and closed his eyes. For a minute or two he convinced himself that the music made it impossible to hear the workmen. First he noticed that if he lay completely still, he could feel a vibration in his arms and legs and then, gradually, the distinctive, steady rising and falling rhythm of steel on concrete, closer, more insistent then ever, returned. He opened his eyes. The cable-suspended platform was at eye level, directly outside his window. One of the two workmen scanned the living room and then looked at Dexter. When he saw that Dexter was looking back, the man averted his eyes and resumed the chiselling action with the hand-held tool.

Dexter thought to close the blinds, but decided his only option was to leave the building. He went to the bedroom and changed into khakis and a short-sleeved cotton shirt and walked to the kitchen to take his keys from the rack inside the door.

When his elevator arrived in the lobby he got off and was halfway to the lounge area when he turned and strode directly to the condominium office. The girl positioned at the first desk smiled. Dexter looked past her to the window and the larger desk occupied by the manager. "I need to see Mrs. Wormser," said Dexter. Mrs. Wormser, on the phone, glanced over then looked out the window.

After ten minutes or so, she hung up, and went to the file cabinets without so much as a nod to Dexter. The receptionist looked first at her supervisor and then at Dexter, but before she could speak, Dexter said in a loud voice: "Mrs. Wormser, if you're not too terribly busy."

The Wormser woman turned slowly and held up her hand. "Yes, Mr. Giles. I see you. In a moment. Please."

When at last she closed the file cabinet and walked over to him, he said, "Tell me, where is the logic in hiring two workmen to refit the exterior of a forty-storey building? At their pace they won't be finished by December."

"These are necessary repairs; the logic is dictated by our budget. You receive a copy of the financials."

"And I know there's enough reserved to hire a reputable contractor. Have you taken a good look at the truck these guys drive? I've seen newer ones in the Museum of Science and Industry." At this the receptionist stifled a laugh and Mrs. Wormser pretended not to notice.

"If you don't approve of the way we do things, I suggest you attend the association meetings. With your vast knowledge of business you could demonstrate to us the error of our ways."

On his way out of the building Dexter looked to the curb at the contractor's dilapidated truck. The paint had oxidized and rusted to such an extent that it was no longer possible to determine the vehicle's original color. And the treadless tires needed air.

Heat radiated off the street; impatiens drooped in the humidity. Dexter crossed Sheridan Road, continued east on Diversey. As he passed the supermarket on the opposite side of the street he glanced over, with the thought of buying earplugs, and noticed the woman going inside. From the back she looked like Tula, except her hair was black. Without thinking he stopped walking and stood and gazed across at the entrance for a moment. She hadn't phoned since their rift on the way home from Springfield more than three weeks ago. He continued ahead, went into the coffee bar, and ordered a grande espresso, then took a seat at a table on the sidewalk. Sipping slowly, he trained his eyes on the automatic doors of the market and waited.

Gallagher himself had called to tell her of his wife's death. And yes she had agreed to attend the service in the south Chicago suburb. She had in fact taken Gallagher's call only moments after Dexter's invitation to drive to Springfield.

"Naturally you'll be his date for the funeral," Dexter had said. "Such a glorious occasion calls for a new dress. Have you decided on black or red?"

"You're a bitter queen," said Tula.

"You're the one who said you'd spit in his face. You did say spit, didn't you?" said Dexter.

After ten minutes he saw Tula come out. She had indeed changed her hair color, back to waitress-black. She walked west towards Clark and Broadway, moving purposefully with her head down, at a brisk pace. Dexter swallowed the last of his espresso and walked back to his apartment.

***

September passed slowly, but once the work on the building ceased and quiet returned to Dexter's apartment, the passing of October days seemed more bearable. Halloween was two days away. Dexter listened to the Beethoven Seventh Symphony while he tidied the living room. During the coda he straightened and peered out over the lake. The contrast of the joyful music coexisting with the ominous rumbling in the bass section seemed the perfect expression of his life in retirement. Despite the occasional surge of contentment, gloom and foreboding tugged in parallel, from deep inside, to remind him that life, his life anyway, had no purpose.

After the music ended he turned off the stereo and went to the kitchen. When the telephone rang, he dismissed it as a sales call, then answered and was surprised to hear Tula's voice.

"Did you think I'd died?"

"You probably hoped I had," said Dexter.

"I'd like. to see you. Are you free for dinner tomorrow night?"

***

Tula hadn't said much on the phone, insisting she was in a rush to get out of her house and get to the cleaners.

She was already waiting at the restaurant when Dexter arrived. Her complexion flushed and she smiled. "I guess I should start at the beginning," she said. "Jim Gallagher and I are getting married. It's going to be a small ceremony for friends and family, and I want you to come."

Dexter had already seen the ring. He rested his forehead in his hand for a moment. "Congratulations. I'm happy for you," he said.

Tears formed in her eyes, when Dexter apologized for the things he had said on the way home from Springfield, and then he allowed Tula to really start at the beginning. She had gone to the funeral home service for Louise Gallagher and had been surprised at the extent that Jim had aged. The liver spots on his hands especially brought her attention to how much time had elapsed since they'd been intimate. He had cried so. And at one point, after everyone but family had left, he had put his arms around her and wept with her. "I'm so sorry, Tu," he had said again and again. She hadn't been able to get him out of her mind. He'd been so strong and impregnable during their years together at Imperial. He had called her the following week before returning to Florida and invited her to dinner at his daughter's house. And then he had showed up unannounced one day at her house and invited her for a drive.

When he returned to Florida he called her every day and begged her to come and visit. Finally after much soul-searching she had forgiven him and made a reservation for Florida. She spent almost an entire month.

Dexter knew that after Gallagher regained his confidence and strength he would want more. There had been others, besides Tula. Gallagher's reputation for sexual liaisons in foreign ports had been well-known. Dexter wondered if she and Jim still had sexual relations. Tula would manage business affairs—Gallagher still owned the rental property in Key Biscayne—and keep house, while he spent afternoons at the country club playing golf and entertaining his cronies with Imperial war stories.

Who was to say that he himself wouldn't accept an opportunity for companionship. The sun was low, but it was hot for late October. By the time he reached Sheridan Road, Dexter's clothes, damp with sweat, clung to his body, but he attributed it to the large meal and glasses of wine he had consumed.

Traffic at the intersection was jammed, and drivers honked their horns. When the *walk* signal came on and the crossing cleared of cars, Dexter saw the woman sitting in the street. He ran to her and reached to help her to her feet, but she merely looked at him and pulled her shopping bag in close. She was quite thin, dressed in a black, silk pantsuit and a straw, coolie hat. Only her bony hands and white withered face were exposed. Gradually he got her to her feet and led her to the curb. He asked where she lived, but she didn't reply. Several times he said, "Are you able to continue?" and he offered to accompany her. Once back on the sidewalk, aloof and still silent, she faced north and pulled her arm from his grasp. Clutching her shopping bag ever closer, she resumed her deliberate journey up the street.

Dexter hadn't bothered to ask about Tula's mother. No doubt she would be left behind in the nursing home.

About the Author

Ronald Alexander's work has appeared in publications including *Chicago Tribune*, *New Mexico Humanities Review*, *The James White Review*, *Columbia*, *The Chattahoochee Review*, and *Confrontation*. He lives in Venice, California.